THE FACE OF FEAR

Also by Dean R Koontz

Midnight
The Mask
Lightning
Watchers
Whispers
Night Chills
Darkness Comes
Phantoms
The Vision
The Voice of the Night
Chase
Shattered
Twilight Eyes

THE FACE OF FEAR

Dean R Koontz

HEADLINE

First published in Great Britain in 1978
by Peter Davies Limited
as THE FACE OF FEAR by K R Dwyer

Reprinted in 1989
by HEADLINE BOOK PUBLISHING PLC

British Library Cataloguing in Publication Data

Koontz, Dean R. *1945–*
The face of fear.
I. Title
813′54 [F]

ISBN 0–7472–0174–9

Typeset by Colset Private Limited, Singapore

Printed and bound in Great Britain by
Mackays of Chatham PLC, Chatham, Kent

HEADLINE BOOK PUBLISHING
A division of Hodder Headline PLC
338 Euston Road
London NW1 3BH

For Barbara Norville

Part one

FRIDAY

12:01 A.M. – 8:00 P.M.

1

Wary, not actually expecting trouble but prepared for it, he parked his car across the street from the four-story brownstone apartment house. When he switched off the engine, he heard a siren wail in the street behind him.

They're coming for me, he thought. Somehow they've found out I'm the one.

He smiled. He wouldn't let them put the handcuffs on him. He wouldn't go easily. That wasn't his style.

Frank Bollinger was not easily frightened. In fact, he couldn't remember *ever* having been frightened. He knew how to take care of himself. He had reached six feet when he was thirteen years old, and he hadn't quit growing until he was six-four. He had a thick neck, broad shoulders and the biceps of a young weightlifter. At thirty-seven he was in virtually the same good condition, at least outwardly, as he had been when he was twenty-seven – or even seventeen. Curiously enough, he never exercised. He had neither the time nor the temperament for endless series of push-ups and sit-ups and running in place. His size and his hard-packed muscles were nature's gifts, simply a matter of genetics. Although he had a voracious appetite and never dieted, he was not girdled with rings of extra weight in the hips and stomach, as were most men his age. His doctor had explained to him that, because he suffered constantly from extreme nervous tension and because he refused to take the drugs that would bring his condition under control, he would most likely die young of hypertension. Strain, anxiety, nervous tension – these were what kept the weight off him, said the doctor. Wound tight, roaring inside like a perpetually accelerating engine, he burned away the fat, regardless of how much he ate.

But Bollinger found that he could agree with only half of that diagnosis. Nervous: no. Tension: yes. He was never nervous; that word had no meaning for him. However, he was always tense. He *strove* for tension, worked at building it, for he thought of it as a survival factor. He was always watchful. Always aware. Always tense. Always ready. Ready for anything. That was why there was nothing that he feared: nothing on earth could surprise him.

As the siren grew louder, he glanced at the rearview mirror. A bit more than a block away, a revolving red light pulsed in the night.

He took the .38 revolver out of his shoulder holster. He put one hand on the door and waited for the right moment to throw it open.

The squad car bore down on him – then swept past. It turned the corner two blocks away.

They weren't on his trail after all.

He felt slightly disappointed.

He put the gun away and studied the street. Six mercury vapor street lamps – two at each end of the block and two in the middle – drenched the pavement and the automobiles and the buildings in an eerie purple-white light. The street was lined with three- and four-story town houses, some of them brownstones and some brick, most of them in good repair. There didn't seem to be anyone at any of the lighted windows. That was good; he did not want to be seen. A few trees struggled for life at the edges of the sidewalks, the scrawny plane trees and maples and birches that were all that New York City could boast beyond the boundaries of its public parks, all of them stunted trees, skeletal, their branches like charred bones reaching for the midnight sky. A gentle but chilly January wind pushed scraps of paper along the gutters; and when the wind gusted, the branches of the trees rattled like children's sticks on a rail fence. The other parked cars looked like animals huddling against the cold air; they were empty. Both sidewalks were deserted for the length of the block.

He got out of the car, quickly crossed the street and went up the front steps of the apartment house.

The foyer was clean and brightly lighted. The complex mosaic floor – a garland of faded roses on a beige background – was highly polished, and there were no pieces of tile missing from it. The inner foyer door was locked and could only be opened by key or with a lock-release button in one of the apartments.

There were three apartments on the top floor, three on the second floor and two on the ground level. Apartment 1A belonged to Mr and Mrs Harold Nagly, the owners of the building, who were on their annual pilgrimage to Miami Beach. The small apartment at the rear of the first floor was occupied by Edna Mowry, and he supposed that right now Edna would be having a midnight snack or a well-deserved martini to help her relax after a long night's work.

He had come to see Edna. He knew she would be home. He had followed her for six nights now, and he knew that she lived by strict routine, much too strict for such a young and attractive woman. She always arrived home from work at twelve, seldom more than five minutes later.

Pretty little Edna, he thought. You've got such long and lovely legs.

He smiled.

He pressed the call button for Mr and Mrs Yardley on the third floor.

A man's voice echoed tinnily from the speaker at the top of the mailbox. 'Who is it?'

'Is this the Hutchinson apartment?' Bollinger asked, knowing full well that it was not.

'You pressed the wrong button, mister. The Hutchinsons are on the second floor. Their mailbox is next to ours.'

'Sorry,' Bollinger said as Yardley broke the connection.

He rang the Hutchinson apartment.

The Hutchinsons, apparently expecting visitors and less cautious than the Yardleys, buzzed him through the inner door without asking who he was.

The downstairs hall was pleasantly warm. The brown tile floor and tan walls were spotless. Halfway along the corridor, a marble bench stood on the left, and a large beveled mirror hung above it. Both apartment doors, dark wood with brassy fixtures, were on the right.

He stopped in front of the second door and flexed

his gloved fingers. He pulled his wallet from an inside coat pocket and took a knife from an overcoat pocket. When he touched the button on the burnished handle, the spring-hinged blade popped into sight; it was seven inches long, thin and nearly as sharp as a razor.

The gleaming blade transfixed Bollinger and caused bright images to flicker behind his eyes.

He was an admirer of William Blake's poetry; indeed, he fancied himself an intimate spiritual student of Blake's. It was not surprising, then, that a passage from Blake's work should come to him at that moment, flowing through his mind like blood running down the troughs in an autopsy table.

Then the inhabitants of those cities
Felt their nerves change into marrow,
And the hardening bones began
In swift diseases and torments,
In shootings and throbbings and grindings
Through all the coasts; till, weakened,
The senses inward rushed, shrinking
Beneath the dark net of infection.

I'll change their bones to marrow, sure as hell, Bollinger thought. I'll have the inhabitants of *this* city hiding behind their doors at night. Except that I'm not the infection; I'm the cure. I'm the cure for all that's wrong with this world.

He rang the bell. After a moment he heard her on the other side of the door, and he rang the bell again.

'Who is it?' she asked. She had a pleasant, almost musical voice, marked now with a thin note of apprehension.

'Miss Mowry?' he asked.

'Yes?'

'Police.'

She didn't reply.

'Miss Mowry? Are you there?'

'What's it about?'

'Some trouble where you work.'

'I never cause trouble.'

'I didn't say that. The trouble doesn't involve you. At least not directly. But you might have seen something important. You might have been a witness.'

'To what?'

'That will take a while to explain.'

'I couldn't have been a witness. Not me. I wear blinders in that place.'

'Miss Mowry,' he said sternly, 'if I must get a warrant in order to question you, I will.'

'How do I know you're really the police?'

'New York,' Bollinger said with mock exasperation. 'Isn't it just wonderful? Everyone suspects everyone else.'

'They have to.'

He sighed. 'Perhaps. Look, Miss Mowry, do you have a security chain on the door?'

'Of course.'

'Of course. Well, leave the chain on and open up. I'll show you my identification.'

Hesitantly, she slid back a bolt lock. The chain lock allowed the door to open an inch and no farther.

He held up his wallet. 'Detective Bollinger,' he said. The knife was in his left hand, pointed at the floor, pressed flat against his overcoat.

She squinted through the narrow crack. She peered for a moment at the badge that was pinned to the inside of his wallet, then carefully studied the photo-identification card in the plastic window below the badge.

When she stopped squinting at the ID and looked up at him, he saw that her eyes were not blue, as he had thought - having seen her no closer than when she was on stage and he was in the shadowed audience - but a deep shade of green. They were truly the most attractive eyes he had ever seen. 'Satisfied?' he asked.

Her thick dark hair had fallen across one eye. She pushed it away from her face. Her fingers were long and perfectly formed, the nails painted blood red. When she was on stage, bathed in that intense spotlight, her nails appeared to be black. She said, 'What's this trouble you mentioned?'

'I have quite a number of questions to ask you, Miss Mowry. Must we discuss this through a crack in the door for the next twenty minutes?'

Frowning, she said, 'I suppose not. Wait there just a minute while I put on a robe.'

'I can wait. Patience is the key to content.'

She looked at him curiously.

'Mohammed,' he said.

'A cop who quotes Mohammed?'

'Why not?'

'Are you - of that religion?'

'No.' He was amused at the way she phrased the question. 'It's just that I've acquired a considerable amount of knowledge for the sole purpose of shocking those people who think all policemen are hopelessly ignorant.'

She winced. 'Sorry.' Then she smiled. He had not seen her smile before, not once in the entire week since he had first seen her. She had stood in that spotlight, moving with the music, shedding her clothes, bumping, grinding, caressing her own bare breasts, observing her audience with the cold eyes and almost lipless expression of a snake. Her smile was dazzling.

'Get your robe, Miss Mowry'

She closed the door.

Bollinger watched the foyer door at the end of the hall, hoping no one would come in or go out while he was standing there, exposed.

He put away his wallet.

He kept the knife in his left hand.

In less than a minute she returned. She removed the security chain, opened the door and said, 'Come in.'

He stepped past her, inside.

She closed the door and put the bolt lock in place and turned to him and said, 'Whatever trouble –'

Moving quickly for such a large man he slammed her against the door, brought up the knife, shifted it from his left hand to his right hand, and lightly pricked her throat with the point of the blade.

Her green eyes were very wide. She'd had the breath knocked out of her and could not scream.

'No noise,' Bollinger said fiercely. 'If you try to call for help, I'll push this pig sticker straight into your lovely throat. I'll ram it right out the back of your neck. Do you understand?'

She stared at him.

'*Do you understand?*'

'Yes,' she said thinly.

'Are you going to cooperate?'

She said nothing. Her gaze traveled down from his eyes, over his proud nose and full lips and strong jawline, down to his fist and to the handle of the knife.

'If you aren't going to cooperate,' he said quietly, 'I can skewer you right here. I'll pin you to the damn door.' He was breathing hard.

A tremor passed through her.

He grinned.

Still trembling, she said, 'What do you want?'

'Not much. Not very much at all. Just a little loving.'

She closed her eyes. 'Are you – him?'

A slender, all but invisible thread of blood trickled from beneath the needlelike point of the knife, slid along her throat to the neck of her bright red robe. Watching the minuscule flow of blood as if he were a scientist observing an extremely rare bacterium through a microscope, pleased by it, nearly mesmerized by it, he said, 'Him? Who is "him"? I don't know what you're talking about.'

'You know,' she said weakly.

'I'm afraid not.'

'Are you *him*?' she bit her lip. 'The one who – who's cut up all those other women?'

Looking up from her throat, he said, 'I see. I see how it is. Of course. You mean the one they call the Butcher. You think I'm the Butcher.'

'Are you?'

'I've been reading a great deal about him in the *Daily News*. He slits their throats, doesn't he? From one ear to the other. Isn't that right?' He was teasing her and enjoying himself immensely. 'Sometimes he even disembowels them. Doesn't he? Correct me if I'm wrong. But that's what he does sometimes, isn't it?'

She said nothing.

'I believe I read in the *News* that he sliced the

ears off one of them. When the police found her, her ears were on the nightstand beside her bed.'

She shuddered more violently than ever.

'Poor little Edna. You think I'm the Butcher. No wonder you're so frightened.' He patted her shoulder, smoothed her dark hair as if he were quieting an animal. 'I'd be scared too if I were in your shoes right now. But I'm not. I'm not in your shoes and I'm not this guy they call the Butcher. You can relax.'

She opened her eyes and searched his, trying to tell whether he spoke the truth.

'What kind of man do you think I am, Edna?' he asked, pretending to have been hurt by her suspicion. 'I don't want to harm you. I will if I must. I will cause you a great deal of harm if you don't cooperate with me. But if you're docile, if you're good to me, I'll be good to you. I'll make you very happy, and I'll leave you just like I found you. Flawless. You are flawless, you know. Perfectly beautiful. And your breath smells like strawberries. Isn't that nice? That's such a wonderful way for us to begin, such a nice touch, that scent of strawberries on your breath. Were you eating when I knocked?'

'You're crazy,' she said softly.

'Now, Edna, let's have cooperation. Were you eating strawberries?'

Tears began to form in the corners of her eyes.

He pressed a bit harder with the knife.

She whimpered.

'Well?' he said.

'Wine.'

'What?'

'It was wine.'

'Strawberry wine?'

'Yes.'

'Is there any left?'

'Yes.'

'I'd like to have some.'

'I'll get it for you.'

'I'll get it myself,' he said. 'But first I've got to take you into the bedroom and tie you up. Now, now. Don't be scared. If I didn't tie you up, sooner or later you'd try to escape. If you tried to escape, I'd have to kill you. So, you see, I'm going to tie you up for your own good, so that you won't make it necessary for me to hurt you.'

Still holding the knife at her throat, he kissed her. Her lips were cold and stiff.

'Please don't,' she said.

'Relax and enjoy yourself, Edna.' He untied the sash at her waist. The robe fell open. Under it, she was naked. He gently squeezed her breasts. 'If you cooperate you'll come out of this just fine. And you'll have a lot of fun. I'm not going to kill you unless you force me to it. I'm no butcher, Edna. Me . . . I'm nothing but your ordinary, everyday rapist.'

Graham Harris sensed ... coming. He shifted in ... get comfortable. He glanced ... cameras and suddenly ... intelligent and hostile ... at that bizarre ... slightly giddy.

'Nervous?' Anthony Prime ...

'A little.'

'No need to be.'

'Maybe not while the ...

...'

'Not when we're ...' Prime said. 'You're ...' Although he was ... managed to look like ... gentleman: sophisticated, ... bit stuffy, completely ... confidence. He was sitting in ... leather armchair, an exact copy of ... which Graham had suddenly found ... uncomfortable. 'You're ... Mr Harris.'

'Thank you. You're ...

2

Graham Harris sensed that there was trouble coming. He shifted in his chair but could not get comfortable. He glanced at the three television cameras and suddenly felt as if he were surrounded by intelligent and hostile robots. He almost laughed at that bizarre image; the tension made him slightly giddy.

'Nervous?' Anthony Prine asked.

'A little.'

'No need to be.'

'Maybe not while the commercials are running, but –'

'Not when we're back on the air again, either,' Prine said. 'You've handled yourself well so far.' Although he was as American as Harris, Prine managed to look like the stereotypical British gentleman: sophisticated, rather jaded yet just a bit stuffy, completely relaxed, a model of self-confidence. He was sitting in a high-backed leather armchair, an exact copy of the chair in which Graham had suddenly found himself so uncomfortable. 'You're a most interesting guest, Mr Harris.'

'Thank you. You're interesting yourself. I don't

see how you can keep your wits about you. I mean, doing this much *live* television, five nights a week –'

'But the fact that it's live is what makes it so exciting,' Prine said. 'Being on the air *live*, risking all, taking a chance of making a fool of yourself – that keeps the juices flowing. That's why I hesitate to accept one of these offers to syndicate the show or to go network with it. They'd want it on tape, all neatly edited down from two hours to ninety minutes. And that wouldn't be the same.'

The program director, a heavyset man in a white turtleneck sweater and houndstooth-check slacks, said, 'Twenty seconds, Tony.'

'Relax,' Prine told Harris. 'You'll be off in fifteen more minutes.'

Harris nodded. Prine seemed friendly – yet he could not shake the feeling that the night was going to go sour for him, and soon.

Anthony Prine was the host of *Manhattan at Midnight*, an informal two-hour-long interview program that originated from a local New York City station. *Manhattan at Midnight* provided the same sort of entertainment to be found on all other talk shows – actors and actresses plugging their latest movies, authors plugging their latest books, musicians plugging their latest records, politicians plugging their latest campaigns (as yet unannounced campaigns and thus unfettered by the equal-time provisions of the election laws) – except that it presented a greater number of mind readers and psychics and UFO 'experts' than did most talk shows. Prine was a *Believer*. He was also damned good at his job, so good there were rumors that ABC wanted to pick him up for a nationwide audience. He was not so witty as Johnny Carson or so homey as Mike Douglas, but no one asked better or more probing questions than he did. Most of the time he was serene, in lazy command of his show; and when things were going well, he looked somewhat like a slimmed-down Santa Claus: completely white hair, a round face and merry blue eyes. He appeared to be incapable of rudeness. However, there were occasions - no more often than once a night, sometimes only once a week - when he would lash out at a guest, prove him a liar or in some other way thoroughly embarrass and humiliate him with a series of wickedly pointed questions. The attack never lasted more than three or four minutes, but it was as brutal and as relentless as it was surprising.

Manhattan at Midnight commanded a large and faithful audience primarily because of this element of surprise that magnified the ferocity of Prine's interrogations. If he had subjected every guest to this abuse, he would have been a bore; but his calculated style made him as fascinating as a cobra. Those millions of people who spend most of their leisure hours in front of a television set apparently enjoyed secondhand violence more than they did any other form of entertainment. They watched the police shows to see people beaten, robbed and murdered; they watched Prine for those unexpected moments when he bludgeoned a guest with words that were nearly as devastating as clubs.

He had started twenty-five years earlier as a nightclub comic and impressionist, doing old jokes and mimicking famous voices in cheap lounges. He had come a long way.

The director signaled Prine. A red light shone on one camera.

Addressing his unseen audience, Prine said, 'I'm talking with Mr Graham Harris, a resident of Manhattan who calls himself a "clairvoyant," a seer of visions. Is that the proper definition of the term, Mr Harris?'

'It'll do,' Graham said. 'Although when you put it that way, it sounds a bit religious. Which it isn't. I don't attribute my extrasensory perception to God – nor to any other supernatural force.'

'As you said earlier, you're convinced that the clairvoyance is a result of a head injury you received in a rather serious accident. Subsequent to that, you began to have these visions. If that's God's work, His methods are even more roundabout than we might have thought.'

Graham smiled. 'Precisely.'

'Now, anyone who reads the newspapers knows that you've been asked to assist the police in uncovering a clue to the identity of this man they call the Butcher. But what about your last case, the murder of the Havelock sisters in Boston? That was very interesting too. Tell us about that.'

Graham shifted uneasily in his chair. He still sensed trouble coming, but he couldn't imagine what it might be or how he might avoid it 'The Havelock sisters . . .'

Nineteen-year-old Paula and twenty-two-year-old Paige Havelock had lived together in a cozy Boston apartment near the university where Paula was an undergraduate student and where Paige was working for her master's degree in sociology. On the morning of last November second, Michael Shute had stopped by the apartment to take Paige to lunch. The date had been made by telephone the previous evening. Shute and the elder Havelock sister were lovers, and he had a key to the apartment. When no one responded to the bell, he decided to let himself in and wait for them. Inside, however, he discovered that they *were* at home. Paula and Paige had been awakened in the night by one or more intruders who had stripped them naked; pajamas and robes were strewn on the floor. The women had been tied with a heavy cord, sexually molested and finally shot to death in their own living room.

Because the proper authorities were unable to come up with a single major lead in the case, the parents of the dead girls got in touch with Graham on the tenth of November and asked for his assistance. He arrived in Boston two days later. Although the police were skeptical of his talents – a number of them were downright hostile toward him – they were anxious to placate the Havelocks, who had some political influence in the city. He was taken to the sealed apartment and permitted to examine the scene of the crime. But he got absolutely nothing from that: no emanations, no psychic visions – just a chill that slithered down his spine and coiled in his stomach. Later, under the suspicious gaze of a police property officer, he was allowed to handle the pillow that the killer had used to muffle the gunshots – and then the pajamas and the robes that had been found next to the bodies. As he caressed the blood-stiffened fabric, his paranormal talent abruptly blossomed; his mind was inundated with clairvoyant images like a series of choppy, frothing waves breaking on a beach.

Anthony Prine interrupted Graham. 'Wait a minute. I think we need some elaboration on this point. We need to make it much clearer. Do you mean that the simple act of touching the blood-stained pajamas caused your clairvoyant visions?'

'No. It didn't cause them. It *freed* them. The pajamas were like a key that unlocked the clairvoyant part of my mind. That's a quality common to nearly all murder weapons and to the last garments worn by the victims.'

'Why do you think that is?'

'I don't know,' Graham said.

'You've never thought about it?'

'I've thought about it endlessly,' Graham said. 'But I've never reached any conclusions.'

Although Prine's voice held not even the slightest note of hostility, Graham was almost certain that the man was searching for an opening to launch one of his famous attacks.

For a moment he thought *that* might be the oncoming trouble which he had known about, in a somewhat psychic fashion, for the past quarter of an hour. Then he suddenly understood, through the powers of his sixth sense, that the trouble would happen to someone else, beyond the walls of this studio.

'When you touched the pajamas,' Prine said, 'did you see the murders as if they were actually taking place in front of you at that very moment?'

'Not exactly. I saw it all take place - well, *behind* my eyes.'

'What do you mean by that? Are your visions sort of like daydreams?'

'In a way. But much more vivid than daydreams. Full of color and sound and texture.'

'Did you see the Havelocks' killer in this vision?'

'Yes. Quite clearly.'

'Did you also intuit his name?'

'No,' Graham said. 'But I was able to give the police a thorough description of him. He was in his early thirties, not shorter than five-ten or taller than six feet. Slightly heavy. Receding hairline. Blue eyes. A thin nose, generally sharp features. A small strawberry birthmark on his chin . . . As it turned out, that was a perfect description of the building superintendent.'

'And you'd never seen him?'

'My first glimpse of him was in that vision.'

'You'd never seen a photograph of him?'

'No.'

'Had he been a suspect before you gave the police this description?' Prine asked.

'Yes. But the murders took place in the early morning hours of his day off. He swore that he had gone to his sister's house to spend the night, hours before the Havelock girls were killed; and his sister supported his story. Since she lived over eighty miles away, he seemed out of the running.'

'Was his sister lying?'

'Yes.'

'How did you prove it?'

While handling the dead girls' clothing, Graham sensed that the killer had gone to his sister's house a full two hours after the murder had taken place – not early the previous evening as she insisted. He also sensed that the weapon – a Smith & Wesson Terrier .32 – was hidden in the sister's house, in the bottom drawer of a china closet.

He accompanied a Boston city detective and two state troopers to the sister's place. Arriving unannounced and uninvited, they told her they wanted to question her on some new evidence in the case. Ten seconds after he stepped into her house, while the woman was still surprised at the sight of them, Graham asked her why she had said that her brother had come to stay on the evening of November first when in fact he actually had not arrived until well after dawn on November second. Before she could answer that, before she could get her wits about her, he asked her why she was hiding the murder weapon in the bottom drawer of her china closet. Shocked by his knowledge, she withstood only half a dozen questions from the detective before she finally admitted the truth.

'Amazing,' Prine said. 'And you had never seen the inside of her house before you had that vision?'

'I'd never even seen the outside of it,' Graham said.

'Why would she protect her brother when she knew he was guilty of such a horrible crime?'

'I don't know. I can see things that have happened – and very occasionally, things that soon will happen – in places where I've never been. But I can't read minds. I can't explain human motivations.'

The program director signaled Prine: five minutes until they broke for the commercials.

Leaning toward Harris, Prine said, 'Who asked you to help catch this man they're calling the Butcher? Parents of one of the murdered women?'

'No. One of the detectives assigned to the case isn't as skeptical as most policemen. He believes that I can do what I say I can do. He wants to give me a chance.'

'Have you gone to the scenes of the nine murders?'

'I've seen five of them.'

'And handled the clothes of the victims?'

'Some of them.'

Prine slid forward on his chair, leaning conspiratorially toward Harris. 'What can you tell us about the Butcher?'

'Not much,' Graham Harris said, and he frowned, because that bothered him. He was having more trouble than usual on this case. 'He's a big man. Good-looking. Young. Very sure of himself and sure of the –'

'How much are you being paid?' Prine asked.

Confused by the question, Graham said, 'For what?'

'For helping the police,' Prine said.

'I'm not being paid anything.'

'You're just doing it for the good of society, then?'

'I'm doing it because I *have* to. I'm compelled –'

'How much did the Havelocks pay you?'

He realized that Prine had been leaning toward him not conspiratorially but hungrily, like a beast preparing to pounce on its prey. His hunch had been correct: that son of a bitch had chosen him for the nightly trouncing. But *why*?

'Mr Harris?'

Graham had temporarily forgotten the cameras (and the audience beyond), but now he was uncomfortably aware of them again. 'The Havelocks didn't pay me anything.'

'You're certain of that?'

'Of course I'm certain.'

'You *are* sometimes paid for your services, aren't you?'

'No. I earn my living by –'

'Sixteen months ago a young boy was brutally murdered in the Midwest. We'll skip the name of the town to spare the family publicity. His mother asked for your assistance in uncovering the killer. I spoke with her yesterday. She says that she paid you slightly more than one thousand dollars – and then you failed to find the killer.'

What the hell is he trying to prove? Graham wondered. He knows I'm far from poor. He knows I don't need to run halfway across the country to hustle a few hundred dollars. 'First of all, I *did* tell them who killed the child and where they could look for the evidence that would make their case. But both the police and this woman refused to follow up on the lead that I gave them.'

'Why would they refuse?'

'Because the man I fingered for the murder is the son of a wealthy family in that town. He's also a respected clergyman in his own right, and the stepfather of the dead boy.'

Prine's expression was proof enough that the woman had not told him this part of it. Nevertheless, he pressed the attack. That was uncharacteristic of him. Ordinarily, he was vicious with a guest only when he *knew* that he had evidence enough to ruin him. He was not entirely an admirable man; however, he usually didn't make mistakes. 'But she did pay you the thousand dollars?'

'That was for my expenses. Airline fares, car rentals, meals and lodging while I was working on the case.'

Smiling as if he had made his point, Prine said, 'Do they usually pay your expenses?'

'Naturally. I can't be expected to travel all about, spending thousands of my own money for –'

'Did the Havelocks pay you?'

'My expenses.'

'But didn't you just tell us a minute ago that the Havelocks didn't pay you anything?'

Exasperated, Graham said, 'They didn't *pay* me. They just reimbursed me for –'

'Mr Harris, forgive me if I seem to be accusing you of something you haven't done. But it occurs to me that a man with your reputation for performing psychic miracles could easily take many thousands of dollars a year from the gullible. If he was unscrupulous, that is.'

'Look here –'

'When you're on one of these investigations, do you ever pad your expenses?' Prine asked.

Graham was stunned. He slid forward on his chair, leaned toward Prine. 'That's outrageous!' He realized that Prine had settled back and crossed his legs the instant that he got a strong reaction. That was a clever maneuver that made Graham's response seem exaggerated. He suddenly felt as if *he* were the predator. He supposed that his justifiable indignation looked like the desperate and weak self-defense of a guilty man. 'You know I don't need the money. I'm not a millionaire, but I'm well fixed. My father was a successful publisher. I received a substantial trust fund. Furthermore, I've got a moderately successful business of my own.'

'I know you publish two expensive magazines about mountain climbing,' Prine said. 'But they *do* have small circulations. As for the trust fund . . . I hadn't heard about that.'

He's lying, Graham thought. He prepares meticulously for these shows. When I walked into this studio, he knew almost as much about me as I know about myself. So why is he lying? What will he gain by slandering me? What in hell is happening here?

The woman has green eyes, clear and beautiful green eyes, but there is terror in them now, and she stares up at the blade, the shining blade, and she sucks in her breath to scream, and the blade starts its downward arc . . .

The images passed as suddenly as they had come, leaving him badly shaken. He knew that some clairvoyants – including the two most famous, Peter Hurkos and his fellow Dutchman Gerard Croiset – could receive, interpret and catalogue their psychic perceptions while holding an uninterrupted conversation. Only rarely could Graham manage that. Usually he was distracted by the visions. Occasionally, when they had to do with a particularly violent murder, he was so overwhelmed by them that he blanked out reality altogether. The visions were more than an intellectual experience; they affected him emotionally and spiritually as well. For a moment, seeing the green-eyed woman behind his eyes, he had not been *fully* aware of the world around him: the television audience, the studio, the cameras, Prine. He was trembling.

'Mr Harris?' Prine said.

He looked up from his hands.

'I asked you a question,' Prine said.

'I'm sorry. I didn't hear it.'

As the blood explodes from her throat and her scream dies unborn, he pulls the blade free and raises it high and brings it down, down again, with all of his strength, down between her bare breasts, and he neither scowls nor grins, and he does not laugh maniacally, but goes about the killing in a workmanlike manner, as if this is his profession, as if this is just a job, as if this is no different from a man selling cars for a living or washing windows, merely a task to be finished, stab and rip and tear and bring the blood welling up in pools . . . and then stand up and go home and sleep contentedly, satisfied with a job well done . . .

Graham was shaking uncontrollably. His face was greasy with perspiration, yet he felt as if he were sitting in a cool draft. His own power scared him. Ever since the accident in which he had nearly died, he had been frightened of many things; but these inexplicable visions were the ultimate fear.

'Mr Harris?' Prine said. 'Are you feeling all right?'

The second wave of impressions had lasted only three or four seconds, although it had seemed much longer than that. During that time he was totally unaware of the studio and the cameras.

'He's doing it again,' Graham said softly. 'Right now, this minute.'

Frowning, Prine said, 'Who? Doing what?'

'Killing.'

'You're talking about – the Butcher?'

Graham nodded and licked his lips. His throat was so dry that it hurt him a bit to speak. There was an unpleasant metallic taste in his mouth.

Prine was excited. He faced one of the cameras and said, 'Remember, New York, you heard it and saw it here first.' He turned back to Graham and said, 'Who is he killing?' He was suddenly charged with ghoulish anticipation.

'A woman. Green eyes. Pretty.'

'What's her name?'

Perspiration trickled into the corners of

Graham's eyes and stung them. He wiped his forehead with the back of his hand – and wondered how foolish he looked to the hundreds of thousands who were watching.

'Can you tell me her name?' Prine asked.

Edna . . . pretty little Edna . . . poor little Edna . . . .

'Edna,' Graham said.

'Last name?'

'I don't . . . can't see it.'

'Try. You must try.'

'Maybe . . . dancer.'

'Edna Dancer?'

'I don't . . . maybe not . . . maybe the dancer part isn't right . . . maybe just . . . just the Edna . . .'

'Reach for it,' Prine said. 'Try harder. Can't you force it out?'

'No use.'

'*His* name?'

'Daryl . . . no . . . Dwight.'

'Like Dwight Eisenhower?'

'I'm not certain that's actually his first name . . . or even first or last . . . but people have called him that . . . Dwight . . . yes . . . and he's answered to it.'

'Incredible,' Prine said, apparently having forgotten that he had been in the process of destroying his guest's reputation. 'Do you see his other name, first or last?'

'No. But I sense . . . the police already know him . . . somehow . . . and they . . . they know him well.'

'You mean that he's already a suspect?' Prine asked.

The cameras seemed to move in closer.

Graham wished they would go away. He wished Prine would go away. He should never have come here tonight. Most of all, he wished his clairvoyant powers would go away, vanish back into that lockbox, deep within his mind, from which they had been sprung by the accident.

'I don't know,' Graham said. 'I suppose . . . he must be a suspect. But whatever the situation . . . they know him. They –' He shuddered

'What is it?' Prine asked.

'Edna . . .'

'Yes?'

'She's dead now.'

Graham felt as if he were going to be sick.

'*Where* did it happen?' Prine asked.

Graham sank back in his armchair, struggling to keep control of himself. He felt almost as if he were Edna, as if the knife had been plunged into him.

'Where was she murdered?' Prine asked again.

'In her apartment.'

'What's the address?'

'I don't know.'

'But if the police could get there in time –'

'I've lost it,' Graham said. 'It's gone. I'm sorry. It's all gone for now.'

He felt cold and hollow inside.

3

3

Shortly before two o'clock in the morning, after a conference on the set with the director, Anthony Prine left the studio and went down the hall to his suite, which served him as office, dressing room and home away from home. Inside, he walked straight to the bar, put two ice cubes in a glass and reached for the bottle of bourbon.

His manager and business partner, Paul Stevenson, was sitting on the couch. He wore expensive, well-tailored clothes. Prine was a smart dresser, and he appreciated that quality in other men. The problem was that Stevenson always destroyed the effect of his outfit with one bizarre accessory. Tonight he was wearing a Savile Row suit – a hard-finished gray worsted with a midnight-blue Thai silk lining – a hand-sewn light blue shirt, maroon tie, black alligator shoes. And bright pink socks – with green clocks on the sides. Like cockroaches on a wedding cake.

For two reasons, Stevenson was a perfect business partner: he had money, and he did what he was told to do. Prine had great respect for the dollar. And he did not believe that anyone lived who had the experience, the intelligence or the right to tell *him* what to do.

'Were there any calls for me on the private line?' Prine asked.

'No calls.'

'You're certain?'

'Of course.'

'You were here all the time?'

'Watching the show on that set,' Stevenson said.

'I was expecting a call.'

'I'm sorry. There wasn't one.'

Prine scowled.

'Terrific show,' Stevenson said.

'Just the first thirty minutes. Following Harris, the other guests looked duller than they were. Did we get viewer calls?'

'Over a hundred, all favorable. Do you believe he really saw the killing take place?'

'You heard the details he gave. The color of her eyes. Her name. He convinced me.'

'Until the next victim's found, you don't know that his details were accurate.'

'They were accurate,' Prine said. He finished his bourbon and refilled his glass. He could drink a great deal of whiskey without becoming drunk. Likewise, when he ate he gorged himself, yet he had never been overweight. He was constantly on the prowl for pretty young women, and when he paid for sex he usually went to bed with two call girls. He was not simply a middle-aged man desperately trying to prove his youth. He *needed* those fuels – whiskey, food and women – in large doses. For most of his life he had been fighting ennui, a deep and abiding boredom with the way the world was. Pacing energetically, sipping his bourbon, he said, 'A green-eyed woman named Edna . . . He's right about that. We'll be reading it in the papers tomorrow.'

'You can't *know* –'

'If you'd been sitting there beside him, Paul, you'd have no doubts about it.'

'But wasn't it odd that he had his "vision" just when you about had him nailed?'

'Nailed for what?' Prine asked.

'Well . . . for taking money. For –'

'If he's ever been paid more than his expenses for that kind of work, I've no proof of it,' Prine said.

Perplexed, Stevenson said, 'Then why did you go after him?'

'I wanted to break him. Reduce him to a babbling, defenseless fool.' Prine smiled.

'But if he wasn't guilty –'

'He's guilty of other things.'

'Like what?'

'You'll know eventually.'

Stevenson sighed. 'You enjoy humiliating them right there on television.'

'Of course.'

'Why?'

'Why not?'

'Is it the sense of power?'

'Not at all,' Prine said. 'I enjoy exposing them as fools because they *are* fools. Most men are fools. Politicians, clergymen, poets, philosophers, businessmen, generals and admirals. Gradually, I'm exposing the leaders in every profession. I'm going to show the ignorant masses that their leaders are as dull-witted as they are.' He swallowed some bourbon. When he spoke again, his voice was hard. 'Maybe someday all those fools will go at one another's throats and leave the world to the few of us who can appreciate it.'

'What are you saying?'

'I spoke English, didn't I?'

'You sound so – bitter.'

'I've got a right to.'

'You? After your success?'

'Aren't you drinking, Paul?'

'No. Tony, I don't understand –'

'I think you should have a drink.'

Stevenson knew when he was expected to change the subject. 'I really don't want a drink.'

'Have you ever gotten blind drunk?'

'No. I'm not much of a drinker.'

'Ever gone to bed with two girls at once?'

'What's that got to do with anything?'

'You don't reach out for life like you should,' Prine said. 'You don't *experience*. You don't get loose enough often enough. That's the only thing wrong with you, Paul – other than your socks.'

Stevenson looked at his feet. 'What's wrong with my socks?'

Prine went to the windows. He didn't look at the bright city beyond but stared instead at his reflection in the glass. He grinned at himself. He felt marvelous. Better than he had felt in weeks, and all thanks to Harris. The clairvoyant had brought some excitement and danger into his life, new purpose and interest. Although Graham Harris didn't know it as yet, he was the most important target of Prine's career. We'll destroy him, Prine thought happily; wipe him out, finish him off for good. He turned to Stevenson. 'Are you certain about the phone? I *must* have gotten a call.'

'No. Nothing.'

'Maybe you stepped out of here for a minute.'

'Tony, *I'm* not a fool. Give me some credit. I was here all the time, and the private line never rang.'

Prine finished his second bourbon. It burned his throat. A welcome and pleasant heat rose in him. 'Why don't you have a drink with me?'

Stevenson stood and stretched. 'No. I've really got to go.'

Prine went to the bar.

'You're drinking those awfully fast, Tony.'

'Celebrating,' Prine said as he added ice and bourbon to his glass.

'Celebrating what?'

'The downfall of another fool.'

[illegible]

Connie Davis was waiting for [illegible]
home to the townhouse [illegible]
Village. She took his co[illegible]

She was pretty. [illegible]
Brunette. Grey eyes [illegible]

She owned a prosp[illegible]
shop on Tenth Street [illegible]
as tough as she was pr[illegible]

For the past eighteen [illegible]
lived together. Their [illegible]
thing to genuine roma[illegible]
ever known.

However, it was [illegible]
doctor and nurse [illegible]
dent five years ago [illegible]
himself. His self-respect [illegible]
was here to help him, for [illegible]
that he understood that [illegible]
important task of her life.

'Where have you been?' [illegible]
two-thirty.

'I had to think. I [illegible]
program?'

'We'll talk about it [illegible]

4

Connie Davis was waiting for Graham when he came home to the townhouse they shared in Greenwich Village. She took his coat and hung it in the closet.

She was pretty. Thirty-four years old. Slender. Brunette. Gray eyes. Proud nose. Wide mouth. Sexy.

She owned a prosperous hole-in-the-wall antique shop on Tenth Street. In business she was every bit as tough as she was pretty.

For the past eighteen months she and Graham had lived together. Their relationship was the closest thing to genuine romance that either of them had ever known.

However, it was more than a romance. She was his doctor and nurse as well as his lover. Since the accident five years ago, he had been losing faith in himself. His self-respect faded year by year. She was here to help him, to heal him. She was not certain that he understood this; but she saw it as the most important task of her life.

'Where have you been?' she asked. 'It's two-thirty.'

'I had to think. I went walking. You saw the program?'

'We'll talk about it. But first you need to get warm.'

'Do I ever. It must be twenty below out there.'

'Go into the study and sit down. Relax,' she said. 'I've got a fire going. I'll bring you a drink.'

'Brandy?'

'What else on a night like this?'

'You're nearly perfect.'

'*Nearly?*'

'Mustn't give you a swelled head.'

'I'm too perfect to be immodest.'

He laughed.

She turned from him and went to the bar at the far end of the living room.

With a sixth sense of her own, she knew that he stared after her for a moment before he left the room. Good. Just as planned. He was *meant* to watch. She was wearing a clinging white sweater and tight blue jeans that accentuated her waistline and her bottom. If he hadn't stared after her, she would have been disappointed. After what he had been through tonight, he needed more than a seat in front of the fireplace and a snifter of brandy. He needed her. Touching. Kissing. Making love. And she was willing - more than willing, delighted - to provide it.

She was not merely plunging into her Earth Mother role again. Unquestionably, she *did* have a tendency to overwhelm her men, to be so excessively affectionate and understanding and dependable that she smothered their self-reliance. However, this affair was different from all the others. She wanted to depend on Graham as much as he depended on her. This time she wanted to receive as much as she gave. He was the first man to whom she had ever responded in quite that fashion. She wanted to make love to him in order to soothe him, but she wanted to soothe herself as well. She had always had strong, healthy sexual drives, but Graham had put a new and sharper edge on her desire.

She carried the glasses of Remy Martin into the den. She sat beside him on the sofa.

After a moment of silence, still staring at the fire, he said, 'Why the interrogation? What was he after?'

'Prine?'

'Who else?'

'You've seen his show often enough. You know what he's like.'

'But he usually has a reason for his attacks. And he's always got proof of what he says.'

'Well, at least you shut him up with your visions of the tenth murder.'

'They were real,' he said.

'I know they were.'

'It was so vivid . . . as if I were right there.'

'Was it bad? Bloody?'

'One of the worst. I saw him . . . ram the knife into her throat and then twist it.' He quickly sipped his brandy.

She leaned against him, kissed him on the cheek.

'I can't figure this Butcher,' he said worriedly. 'I've never had so much trouble getting an image of a killer.'

'You sensed his name.'

'Maybe. Dwight . . . I'm not entirely sure.'

'You've given the police a fairly good description of him.'

'But I can't pick up much more about him,' he said. 'When the visions come and I try to force an image of this man, this Butcher, to the center of them, all I get are waves of . . . evil. Not illness, not an impression of a sick mind. Just overwhelming evil. I don't know how to explain this – but the Butcher isn't a lunatic. At least not in the classical sense. He doesn't kill in a maniacal frenzy.'

'He's chopped up nine innocent women,' Connie said. '*Ten* if you count the one they haven't found yet. He cuts off their ears and fingers sometimes. Sometimes he disembowels them. And you say he isn't *crazy?*'

'He's not a lunatic, not by any definition we have of the word. I'd stake my life on it.'

'Maybe you don't sense mental illness because he doesn't know he's sick. Amnesia –'

'No. No amnesia. No schizophrenia. He's very aware of his murders. He's no Dr Jekyll and Mr Hyde. I'll bet he'd pass any psychiatric examination you'd care to give him, and with flying colors. This isn't easy to explain. But I have the feeling that if he *is* a lunatic, he's a whole new breed. No one's ever encountered anything like him before. I think – dammit, I *know* – he's not even angry or particularly excited when he kills these women. He's just – methodical.'

'You're giving me the shivers.'

'You? I feel as if I've been inside his head. I've got a *chronic* case of shivers.'

A coal popped in the fireplace.

She took hold of his free hand. 'Let's not talk about Prine or the killings.'

'After tonight, how can I not talk about them?'

'You looked wonderful on television,' she said, working him away from the subject.

'Oh, yeah. Wonderful. Sweating, pale, shaking –'

'Not during the visions. Before them. You're a

natural for television. Even for movies. Leading-man type.'

Graham Harris was handsome. Thick reddish-blond hair. Blue eyes, heavily crinkled at the corners. Leathery skin with sharply carved lines from all the years he had spent in an outdoor life. Five-ten; not tall, but lean and hard. He was thirty-eight, yet he still had a trace of boyish vulnerability about him.

'Leading-man type?' he said. He smiled at her. 'Maybe you're right. I'll give up the publishing business and all this messy psychic stuff. I'll go into the movies.'

'The next Robert Redford.'

'Robert Redford? I was thinking maybe the next Boris Karloff.'

'Redford,' Connie insisted.

'Come to think of it, Karloff was a rather elegant-looking man out of makeup. Perhaps I'll try for being the next Wallace Beery.'

'If you're Wallace Beery, then I'm Marie Dressler.'

'Hi, Marie.'

'Do you really have an inferiority complex, or do you cultivate it as part of your charm?'

He grinned, then sipped the brandy. 'Remember that Tugboat Annie movie with Beery and Dressler? Do you think Annie ever went to bed with her husband?'

'Sure!'

'They were always fighting. He lied to her every chance he got – and most of the time he was drunk.'

'But in their own way they *loved* each other,' Connie said. 'They couldn't have been married to anyone else.'

'I wonder what it was like for them. He was such a weak man, and she was such a strong woman.'

'Remember, though, he was always strong when the chips were down: right near the end of the picture, for example.'

'Some good in all of us, huh?'

'He could have been strong from the start. He just didn't respect himself enough.'

Graham stared at the fire. He turned the brandy snifter around and around in his hand.

'What about William Powell and Myrna Loy?' she asked.

'The Thin Man movies.'

'Both of them were strong.' she said. 'That's who we could be. Nick and Nora Charles.'

'I always liked their dog. Asta. Now *that* was a good part.'

'How do you think Nick and Nora made love?' she asked.

'Passionately.'

'But with a lot of fun.'

'Little jokes.'

'That's it.' She took the brandy glass out of his hand and put it on the hearth with her own snifter. She kissed him lightly, teasing his lips with her tongue. 'I bet we could play Nick and Nora.'

'I don't know. It's such a strain making love and being witty at the same time.'

She sat in his lap. She put her arms around his neck and kissed him more fully this time and drew back and smiled when he slid a hand beneath her sweater.

'Nora?' he said.

'Yes, Nicky?'

'Where's Asta?'

'I put him to bed.'

'We wouldn't want him interrupting.'

'He's asleep.'

'Might traumatize the little fella if he saw –'

'I made sure he'd be asleep.'

'Oh?'

'I drugged his Alpo.'

'Such a smart girl.'

'And now *we* belong in bed.'

'Such a *very* smart girl.'

'With a lovely body,' she said.

'Yes, you're ravishing.'

'Am I?'

'Oh, yes.'

'Ravish me, then.'

'With pleasure.'

'I would hope so.'

An hour later he was asle[illegible]
She lay on her side, [illegible]
glow of the bedside lamp.

His experience [illegible]
his features. His [illegible]
tel, there was the [illegible]
intelligence. Throu[illegible]
down good men. But the [illegible]
well, the fear of failing [illegible]
that had grown from [illegible]

During his twenties [illegible]
had been one of the [illegible]
world. He lived for the [illegible]
and the triumph. Nothing [illegible]
half so much as that. He had [illegible]
from the age of thirteen, [illegible]
and more difficult goals [illegible]
he was organizing parties [illegible]
peaks in Europe, Asia and South America. When
he was thirty he led an expedition up the [illegible]
route of Everest, climbed the West [illegible]
the mountain, and returned down the [illegible]. At
thirty-one he tackled the [illegible]
Alpine-style single push [illegible]

5

An hour later he was asleep, but Connie was not. She lay on her side, studying his face in the soft glow of the bedside lamp.

His experience and attitudes were stamped on his features. His toughness shone through clearly, yet there was the boyish quality too. Kindness. Intelligence. Humor. Sensitivity. He was a deep-down *good* man. But the fear shone through as well, the fear of falling, and all of the ugly things that had grown from it.

During his twenties and early thirties, Graham had been one of the best mountain climbers in the world. He lived for the vertical trek, for the risk and the triumph. Nothing else in his life mattered half so much as that. He had been an active climber from the age of thirteen, year by year setting higher and more difficult goals for himself. At twenty-six he was organizing parties to scale the most taxing peaks in Europe, Asia and South America. When he was thirty he led an expedition up the South Col route of Everest, climbed the West Ridge to traverse the mountain, and returned down the South Col. At thirty-one he tackled the Eiger Direct with an Alpine-style single push up the hideously sheer face without using fixed ropes. Accomplishments such as these, his good looks, his wit, and his reputation as a Casanova (exaggerated by both his friends and the press) made him the most colorful and popular figure in mountaineering at that time.

Five years ago, with only a few challenging climbs remaining, he put together a team to assault the most dangerous wall of rock known to man, the Southwest Face of Everest, a route that had never been taken to the top. Two-thirds of the way through the climb, he fell, breaking sixteen bones and suffering internal injuries. He was given first aid in Nepal, then flown to Europe with a doctor and two friends at his side in what everyone assumed would conclude as a death watch. Instead of adding one more outstanding achievement to his record, he spent seven months in a private Swiss clinic. However, the ordeal was not at an end when he left the hospital. This Goliath had not been beaten, and had left this David with a warning: Graham limped.

The doctors told him he could still scale easy cliffs and ridges as a weekend sport if he wished. With sufficient practice he might even learn to compensate for his partially game right leg and move on to more ambitious climbs. Not Eiger. Not Everest, by any route. But there were hundreds of lesser palisades that should interest him.

At first he was convinced that he would be back on Everest within a year. Three times he tried to climb, and three times he was reduced to panic in the first hundred feet of the ascent. Forced to retreat from even the simplest climbs, he quickly saw that Everest or anything remotely like it would most likely scare him to death.

Over the years, that fear had undergone a metamorphosis, had grown and spread like a fungus. His fear of climbing had become a generalized fear that affected every aspect of his life. He was convinced that his inheritance would be lost in bad investments, and he began following the stock market with a nervous interest that made him the bane of his broker. He started his three low-circulation, high-priced mountain-climbing magazines as a hedge against a collapse of the market; and although they were quite profitable, he periodically predicted their demise. He began to see the dread specter of cancer in every cold, case of flu, headache and bout with acid indigestion. His clairvoyance frightened him, and he attempted to deal with it only because he could not run from it. At times the fear intruded between him and Connie in the most intimate moments, leaving him impotent.

Recently he had sunk into a depression far deeper than any that had come before it, and for several days he had seemed unable and unwilling to claw his way out of it. Two weeks ago he had witnessed a mugging, heard the victim's cries for help - and walked away. Five years ago he would have waded into the fight without hesitation. He came home and told Connie about the mugging, belittled himself, called himself names and argued with her when she tried to defend him. She was afraid that he had come to loathe himself, and she knew that for a man like Graham such an attitude would lead inevitably to some form of madness.

She knew that she was not particularly qualified to put him back together again. Because of her strong will, because of her competitive and fiercely self-sufficient nature, she felt that she had done more harm than good to her previous lovers.

She had never thought of herself as a women's liberationist and certainly not as a ball breaker; she simply had been, from the age of consent, sharper and tougher and more self-reliant than most men of her acquaintance. In the past her lovers had been emotionally and intellectually weaker than she. Few men seemed able to accept a woman as anything but an inferior. She had nearly destroyed the man she lived with before Graham, merely by assuming her equality and – in his mind, at least – invalidating the male role he needed to sustain himself.

With Graham's ego in a fragile state, she had to modify her basic personality to an extent she would have thought impossible. It was worth the strain, because she saw the man he had been prior to the accident. She wanted to break his shell of fear and let out the old Graham Harris. What he had once been was what she had hoped for so long to find: a man who was her equal and who would not feel threatened by a woman who was his match. However, while trying to bring that Graham back to life, she had to be cautious and patient, for *this* Graham could be shattered so very easily.

A gust of wind rattled the window.

Although she was warm under the covers, she shivered.

The telephone rang.

Startled, she rolled away from Graham.

The phone was strident. Like the cry of a halidon, it echoed eerily in the room.

She snatched up the receiver to stop the ringing before it woke him. 'Hello?' she said softly.

'Mr Harris, please.'

'Who's calling?'

'Ira Preduski.'

'I'm sorry, but I –'

'Detective Preduski.'

'It's four in the morning,' she said.

'I apologize. Really. I'm sorry. Sincerely. If I've wakened you . . . terrible of me. But, you see, he wanted me to call him immediately if we had any – major developments in the Butcher case.'

'Just a minute.' She looked at Graham.

He was awake, watching her.

She said, 'Preduski.'

He took the receiver. 'Harris speaking.'

A minute later, when he was finished, she hung up for him. 'They found number ten?'

'Yeah.'

'What's her name?' Connie asked.

'Edna. Edna Mowry.'

6

The bedclothes were sodden with blood. The carpet at the right of the bed was marred by a dark stain like a Rorschach blot. Dried blood spotted the wall behind the brass headboard.

Three police lab technicians were working in the room under the direction of the coroner. Two of them were on their hands and knees beside the bed. One man was dusting the nightstand for fingerprints, although he must have known that he would not find any. This was the work of the Butcher, and the Butcher always wore gloves. The coroner was plotting the trajectory of the blood on the wall in order to establish whether the killer was left-handed or right-handed.

'Where's the body?' Graham asked.

'I'm sorry, but they took it to the morgue ten minutes ago,' Detective Preduski said, as if he felt responsible for some inexcusable breach of manners. Graham wondered if Preduski's entire life was an apologia. The detective was quick to take the blame for everything - and to find fault with himself even when he behaved impeccably. He was a nondescript man with a pale complexion and watery brown eyes. In spite of his appearance and his apparent inferiority complex, he was a highly respected member of the Manhattan homicide detail. More than one of the detective's associates had made it clear to Graham that he was working with the best, that Ira Preduski was the top man in the department. 'I held the ambulance as long as I could. You took so much time to get here. Of course I woke you in the dead of night. I shouldn't have done that. And then you probably had to call a cab and wait around for it. I'm so sorry. Now I've probably ruined everything for you. I should have tried to keep the body here just a bit longer. I *knew* you'd want to see it where it was found.'

'That doesn't matter,' Graham said. 'In a sense, I've already had a firsthand look at her.'

'Of course you have,' Preduski said. 'I saw you on the Prine show earlier.'

'Her eyes were green, weren't they?'

'Just as you said.'

'She was found nude?'

'Yes.'

'Stabbed many times?'

'Yes.'

'With a particularly brutal wound in the throat?'

'That's right.'

'He mutilated her, didn't he?'

'Yes.'

'How?'

'Awful thing,' Preduski said. 'I wish I didn't have to tell you. Nobody should have to hear it.' Preduski seemed about to wring his hands. 'He cut a plug of flesh out of her stomach. It's almost like a cork, with her navel in the center of it. Terrible.'

Graham closed his eyes and shuddered. 'This . . . cork . . .' He was beginning to perspire. He felt ill. He wasn't receiving a vision, just a strong sense of what had happened, a hunch that was difficult to ignore. 'He put this cork . . . in her right hand and closed her fingers around it. That's where you found it.'

'Yes.'

The coroner turned away from the blood-spattered wall and stared curiously at Graham.

Don't look at me that way, Graham thought. I don't *want* to know these things.

He would have been delighted if his clairvoyance had allowed him to predict sharp rises in the stock market rather than isolated pockets of maniacal violence. He would have preferred to see the names of winning horses in races not yet run rather than the names of victims in murders he'd never seen committed.

If he could have wished away his powers, he would have done that long ago. But because that was impossible, he felt as if he had a responsibility to develop and interpret his psychic talent. He believed, perhaps irrationally, that by doing so he was compensating, at least in part, for the cowardice that had overwhelmed him these past five years.

'What do you make of the message he left us?' Preduski asked.

On the wall beside the vanity bench there were lines of poetry printed in blood.

Rintah roars and shakes his fires
in the burden'd air;
Hungry clouds swag on the deep

'Have any idea what it means?' Preduski asked.

'I'm afraid not.'

'Recognize the poet?'
'No.'
'Neither do I.' Preduski shook his head sorrowfully. 'I'm not very well educated. I only had one year of college. Couldn't afford it. I read a lot but there's so *much* to read. If I were educated, maybe I'd know whose poetry that is. I should know. If the Butcher takes the time to write it down, it's something important to him. It's a lead. What kind of detective am I if I can't follow up a lead as plain as that?' He shook his head again, clearly disgusted with himself. 'Not a good one. Not a very good one.'
'Maybe it's his own poetry,' Graham said.
'The Butcher's?'
'Maybe.'
'A murderous poet? T.S. Eliot with a homicidal urge?'
Graham shrugged.
'No,' Preduski said. 'A man usually commits this sort of crime because it's the only way he can express the rage inside him. Slaughter releases pressures that have built in him. But a poet can express his feelings with words. No. If it were doggerel, perhaps it could be the Butcher's own verse. But this is too smooth, too sensitive, too good. Anyway, it rings a bell. Way back in this thick head of mine, it rings a bell.' Preduski studied the bloody message for a moment, then turned and went to the bedroom door. It was standing open; he closed it. 'Then there's this one.'
On the back of the door, five words were printed in the dead woman's blood.

a rope over an abyss

'Has he ever left anything like this before?' Graham asked.

'No. I would have told you if he had. But it's not unusual in this sort of crime. Certain types of psychopaths like to communicate with whoever finds the corpse. Jack the Ripper wrote notes to the police. The Manson family used blood to scrawl one-word messages on the walls. "A rope over an abyss." What is he trying to tell us?'

'Is it from the same poem as the other?'

'I haven't the faintest idea.' Preduski sighed, thrust his hands into his pockets. He looked dejected. 'I'm beginning to wonder if I'm *ever* going to catch him.'

The living room of Edna Mowry's apartment was small but not mean. Indirect lighting bathed everything in a relaxing amber glow. Gold velvet drapes. Textured light tan burlap-pattern wallpaper. Plush brown carpet. A beige velour sofa and two matching armchairs. A heavy glass coffee table with brass legs. Chrome and glass shelves full of books and statuary. Limited editions of prints by some fine contemporary artists. It was tasteful, cozy and expensive.

At Preduski's request, Graham settled down in one of the armchairs.

Sarah Piper was sitting on one end of the sofa. She looked as expensive as the room. She was wearing a knitted pantsuit - dark blue with Kelly green piping - gold earrings and an elegant watch as thin as a half dollar. She was no older than twenty-five, a strikingly lovely, well-built blonde, marked by experience.

Earlier she had been crying. Her eyes were puffy and red. She was in control of herself now.

'We've been through this before,' she said.

Preduski was beside her on the couch. 'I know,' he said. 'And I'm sorry. Truly sorry. It's terribly late, too late for this. But there *is* something to be gained by asking the same questions two and even three times. You think you've told me all the pertinent facts. But it's possible you overlooked something. God knows, *I'm* forever overlooking things. This questioning may seem redundant to you, but it's the way I work. I have to go over things again and again to make sure I've done them right. I'm not proud of it. That's just the way I am. Some other detective might get everything he needs the first time he speaks to you. Not me, I'm afraid. It was your misfortune that the call came in while I was on duty. Bear with me. I'll be able to let you go home before much longer. I promise.'

The woman glanced at Graham and cocked her head as if to say, *Is this guy for real?*

Graham smiled.

'How long had you known – the deceased?' Preduski asked.

She said, 'About a year.'

'How well did you know her?'

'She was my best friend.'

'Do you think that in her eyes you were *her* best friend?'

'Sure. I was her only friend.'

Preduski raised his eyebrows. 'People didn't like her?'

'Of course they liked her,' Sarah Piper said. 'What wasn't to like? She just didn't make friends easily. She was a quiet girl. She kept mostly to herself.'

'Where did you meet her?'

'At work.'

'Where is work?'

'You know that. The Rhinestone Palace.'

'And what did she do there?'

'You know that too.'

Nodding, patting her knee in a strictly fatherly manner, the detective said, 'That's correct. I know it. But, you see, Mr Harris doesn't know it. I neglected to fill him in. My fault. I'm sorry. Would you tell him?'

She turned to Graham. 'Edna was a stripper. Just like me.'

'I know the Rhinestone Palace,' Graham said.

'You've been there?' Preduski asked.

'No. But I know it's fairly high class, not like most strip-tease clubs.'

For a moment Preduski's watery brown eyes seemed less out of focus than usual. He stared intently at Graham. 'Edna Mowry was a stripper. How about that?'

He knew precisely what the detective was thinking. On the Prine show he had said that the victim's name might be Edna Dancer. He had not been right – but he had not been altogether wrong either; for although her name was Mowry, *she earned her living as a dancer*.

According to Sarah Piper, Edna had reported for work at five o'clock the previous evening. She performed a ten-minute act twice every hour for the next seven hours, peeling out of a variety of costumes until she was entirely nude. Between acts, dressed in a black cocktail dress, sans bra, she mixed with the customers – mostly men, alone and in groups – hustling drinks in a cautious, demure and stylish way that skipped successfully along the edge of the state's B-girl laws. She had finished her last performance at twenty minutes of twelve and left the Rhinestone Palace no more than five minutes after that.

'You think she came straight home?' Preduski asked.

'She always did,' Sarah said. 'She never wanted to go out and have fun. The Rhinestone Palace was all the night life she could stomach. Who could blame her?'

Her voice wavered, as if she might begin to cry again.

Preduski took her hand and squeezed it reassuringly. She let him hold it, and that appeared to give him an innocent pleasure. 'Did you dance last evening?'

'Yeah. Till midnight.'

'When did you come here?'

'A quarter of three.'

'Why would you be visiting at that hour?'

'Edna liked to sit and read all night. She never went to bed until eight or nine in the morning. I told her I'd stop around for breakfast and gossip. I often did.'

'You've probably already told me . . .' Preduski made a face: embarrassment, apology, frustration. 'I'm sorry. This mind of mine – like a sieve. Did you tell me why you didn't come here at midnight, when you got off work?'

'I had a date,' she said.

Graham could tell from her expression and from the tone of her voice that the 'date' had been a paying customer. That saddened him a bit. He liked her already. He couldn't help but like her. He was receiving low-key waves, threshold psychic vibrations from her; they were very positive, mellow and warm vibrations. She was a damned nice person. He *knew*. And he wanted only pleasant things to happen to her.

'Did Edna have a date tonight?' Preduski asked.

'No. I told you. She came right home.'

'Maybe her boyfriend was waiting for her.'

'She was between boyfriends.'

'Maybe an old boyfriend stopped in to talk.'

'No. When Edna dropped a guy, he *stayed* dropped.'

Preduski sighed, pinched the bridge of his nose, shook his head sadly. 'I hate to have to ask this . . . You were her best friend. But what I'm going to say – please understand I don't mean to put her down. Life is tough. We all have to do things we'd rather not do. I'm not proud of every day of my life. God knows. Don't judge. That's my motto. There's only one crime I can't rationalize away. Murder. I really hate to ask this . . . Well, was she . . . do you think she ever . . .'

'Was she a prostitute?' Sarah asked for him.

'Oh, I wouldn't put it that way! That's such an awful . . . I really meant . . .'

'Don't worry,' she said. She smiled sweetly. 'I'm not offended.'

Graham was amused to see her squeeze the detective's hand. Now *she* was comforting *Preduski*.

'I do some light hooking myself,' Sarah said. 'Not much. Once a week, maybe. I've got to like the guy, and he's got to have two hundred bucks to spare. It's all the same as stripping to me, really. But it wouldn't have been something Edna could do. She was surprisingly straight.'

'I shouldn't have asked. It was none of my business,' said Preduski. 'But it occurred to me that in her line of work there would be a lot of temptation for a girl who needed money.'

'She made eight hundred a week stripping and hustling drinks,' Sarah said. 'She only spent money on her books and apartment. She was socking it in the bank. She didn't need more.'

Preduski was somber. 'But you see why I had to ask? If she opened the door to the killer, he must have been someone she knew, however briefly. That's what puzzles me most about this whole case. How does the Butcher get them to open the door?'

Graham had never thought about that. The dead women were all young, but they were from varied backgrounds. One was a housewife. One was a lawyer. Two were schoolteachers. Three secretaries, one model, one sales clerk . . . How *did* the Butcher get so many different women to open their doors to him late at night?

The kitchen table was littered with the remains of a hastily prepared and hastily eaten meal. Bits of bread. The dried edge of a slice of bologna. Smears of mustard and mayonnaise. Two apple cores. A can of cling peaches empty of everything except an inch of packing syrup. A drumstick gnawed to the bone. Half a doughnut. Three crushed beer cans. The Butcher had been ravenous and sloppy.

'Ten murders,' Preduski said, 'and he always goes to the kitchen for a snack afterward.'

Stifled by the psychic atmosphere of the kitchen, by the incredibly strong, lingering presence of the killer which was nearly as heavy here as it had been in the dead woman's bedroom, Graham could only nod. The mess on the table, in contrast with the otherwise tidy kitchen, disturbed him deeply. The peach can and the beer can were covered with reddish-brown stains; the killer had eaten while wearing his bloody gloves.

Preduski shuffled forlornly to the window by the sink. He stared at the neighboring apartment house. 'I've talked to a few psychiatrists about these feasts he has when he's done the dirty work. As I understand it, there are two basic ways a psychopath will act when he's finished with his victim. Number one, there's Mr Meek. The killing is everything for him, his whole reason for living, the only color and desire in his life. When he's done killing, there's nothing, he's nothing. He goes home and watches television. Sleeps a lot. He sinks into a deep pit of boredom until the pressures build up and he kills again. Number two, there's the man who gets psyched up by the murder. His real excitement comes not during the killing but after it. He'll go straight from the scene of the crime to a bar and drink everyone under the table. His adrenalin is up. His heartbeat is up. He eats like a lumberjack and sometimes picks up whores by the six-pack. Apparently, our man is number two. Except . . .'

'Except what?' Graham asked.

Turning away from the window, Preduski said, 'Seven times he's eaten a big meal in the dead women's own homes. Out the other three times, he's taken the food out of the refrigerator and faked a big meal.'

'Faked it? What do you mean?'

'The fifth murder, the Liedstrom woman,' Preduski said. He closed his eyes and grimaced as if he could still see her body and blood. 'We were aware of his style by then. We checked the kitchen right away. There was an empty pear can on the table, an empty cottage cheese container, the remains of an apple and several other items. But there wasn't a mess. The first four times, he'd been sloppy – like he was tonight. But in the Liedstrom kitchen, he hadn't left a lot of crumbs. No smears of butter or mustard or mayonnaise or ketchup. No bloodstains on the beer cans.'

He opened his eyes and walked to the table. 'We'd found well-gnawed apple cores in two of the first four kitchens.' He pointed at an apple core on the table in front of him. 'Like that one. The lab had even studied the teeth marks on them. But in the Liedstrom kitchen he peeled the apple and removed the center with a corer. The skins and the core were piled neatly on one corner of his dinner plate. That was a change from what we'd seen previously, and it got me thinking. Why had he eaten like a Neanderthal the first four times – and like a gentleman the fifth? I had the forensic boys open the plumbing under the sink and take out the garbage disposal unit. They ran tests on it and found that each of the eight kinds of food on the table had been put through the disposal within the past few hours. In short, the Butcher hadn't taken a bite of anything in the Liedstrom kitchen. He got the food from the refrigerator and tossed it down the drain. Then he set the table so it would *look* as if he'd had a big meal. He did the same thing at the scene of murders seven and eight.'

That sort of behavior struck Graham as particularly eerie. The air in the room seemed suddenly more moist and oppressive than before. 'You said his eating after a murder was part of a psychotic compulsion.'

'Yes.'

'If for some reason he didn't feel that compulsion at the Liedstrom house, why would the bother to fake it?'

'I don't know,' Preduski said. He wiped one slender hand across his face as if he were trying to pull off his weariness. 'It's too much for me. It really is. Much too much. If he's crazy, why isn't he crazy in the same way all of the time?'

Graham hesitated. Then: 'I don't think any court-appointed psychiatrist would find him insane.'

'Say again?'

'In fact, I think even the best psychiatrist, if not informed of the murders, would find this man saner and more reasonable than he would most of us.'

Preduski blinked his watery eyes in surprise. 'Well, hell. He carves up ten women and leaves them for garbage, and you don't think he's crazy?'

'That's the same reaction I got from a lady friend when I told her.'

'I don't wonder.'

'But I'll stick by it. Maybe he *is* crazy. But not in any traditional, recognizable way. He's something altogether new.'

'You sense this?'

'Yes.'

'Psychically?'

'Yes.'

'Can you be more specific?'

'Sorry.'

'Sense anything else?'

'Just what you heard on the Prine show.'

'Nothing new since you came here?'

'Nothing.'

'If he's not insane *at all*, then there's a reason behind the killings,' Preduski said thoughtfully. 'Somehow they're connected. Is that what you're saying?'

'I'm not sure *what* I mean.'

'I don't see how they could be connected.'

'Neither do I.'

'I've been looking for a connection, really looking. I was hoping you could pick up something here. From the bloody bedclothes. Or from this mess on the table.'

'I'm blank,' Harris said. 'That's why I'm positive that either he is sane, or he is insane in some whole new fashion. Usually, when I study or touch an item intimately connected with the murder, I can pick up on the emotion, the mania, the passion behind the crime. It's like leaping into a river of violent thoughts, sensations, images . . . This time all I get is a feeling of cool, implacable, evil *logic*. I've never had so much trouble drawing a lead on this kind of killer.'

'Me either,' Preduski said. 'I never claimed to be Sherlock Holmes. I'm no genius. I work slow. Always have. And I've been lucky. God knows. It's luck more than skill that's kept my arrest record high. But this time I'm having no luck at all. None at all. Maybe it's time for me to be put out to pasture.'

On his way out of the apartment, having left Ira Preduski in the kitchen to ponder the remnants of the Butcher's macabre meal, Graham passed through the living room and saw Sarah Piper. The detective had not yet dismissed her. She was sitting on the sofa, her feet propped on the coffee table. She was smoking a cigarette and staring at the ceiling, smoke spiraling like dreams from her head; her back was to Graham.

The instant he saw her, a brilliant image flashed behind his eyes, intense, breathtaking: *Sarah Piper with blood all over her*.

He stopped. Shaking. Waiting for more.

Nothing.

He strained. Tried to pluck more pictures from the ether.

Nothing. Just her face. And the blood. Gone now as quickly as it had come to him.

She became aware of him. She turned around and said, 'Hi.'

He licked his lips, forced a smile.

'You predicted this?' she asked, waving one hand toward the dead woman's bedroom.

'I'm afraid so.'

'That's spooky.'

'I want to say . . .'

'Yes?'

'It was nice meeting you.'

She smiled too.

'I wish it could have been under other circumstances,' he said, stalling, wondering how to tell her about the brief vision, wondering whether he should tell her at all.

'Maybe we will,' she said.

'What?'

'Meet under other circumstances.'

'Miss Piper . . . be careful.'

'I'm always careful.'

'For the next few days . . . be especially careful.'

'After what I've seen tonight,' she said, no longer smiling, 'you can bet on it.'

Frank Bollinger's [illegible]
ian Museum of [illegible]
bedroom walls were [illegible]
floor polished and [illegible]
room was a museum [illegible]
outside [illegible]
the closets and his [illegible]
white walls and the [illegible]
only furniture was a [illegible]
chair with black cushions [illegible]
and shelves [illegible]
sound equipment [illegible]
straightbacked [illegible]
covered with [illegible]
surprising [illegible]
home, and the [illegible]

At nine o'clock Frank [illegible]
showered, plugged [illegible]
pot of coffee.

He had some [illegible]
Edna Mowry's place [illegible]
ing hours drinking [illegible]
poetry. Halfway through [illegible]
but so happy, very happy [illegible]

7

Frank Bollinger's apartment near the Metropolitan Museum of Art was small and spartan. The bedroom walls were cocoa brown, the wooden floor polished and bare. The only furniture in the room was a queen-size bed, one nightstand and a portable television set. He had built shelves into the closets to hold his clothes. The living room had white walls and the same shining wood floor. The only furniture was a black leather couch, a wicker chair with black cushions, a mirrored coffee table, and shelves full of books. The kitchen held the usual appliances and a small table with two straight-backed chairs. The windows were covered with venetian blinds, no drapes. The apartment was more like a monk's cell than a home, and that was how he liked it.

At nine o'clock Friday morning he got out of bed, showered, plugged in the telephone, and brewed a pot of coffee.

He had come directly to his apartment from Edna Mowry's place and had spent the early morning hours drinking Scotch and reading Blake's poetry. Halfway through the bottle, still not drunk but so happy, very happy, he went to bed and fell asleep reciting lines from *The Four Zoas*. When he awoke five hours later, he felt new and fresh and pure, as if he had been reborn.

He was pouring his first cup of coffee when the telephone rang.

'Hello?'

'Dwight?'

'Yeah.'

'This is Billy.'

'Of course.'

Dwight was his middle name - Franklin Dwight Bollinger - and had been the name of his maternal grandfather, who had died when Frank was less than a year old. Until he met and came to know Billy, until he trusted Billy, his grandmother had been the only one who ever used his middle name. Shortly after his fourth birthday, his father abandoned the family, and his mother discovered that a four-year-old interfered with the hectic social life of a divorcee. Except for a few scattered and agonizing months with his mother - who managed to provide occasional bursts of affection only when her conscience began to bother her - he had spent his childhood with his grandmother. She not only wanted him, she cherished him. She treated him as if he were the focus not just of her own life but of the very rotation of the earth.

'Franklin is such an ordinary name,' his grandmother used to say. 'But *Dwight* . . . well, now, that's *special*. It was your grandfather's name, and he was a wonderful man, not at all like other people, one of a kind. You're going to grow up to be just like him, set apart, set above, more important than others. Let everyone call you Frank. To me you'll always be Dwight.' His grandmother had died ten years ago. For nine and a half years no one had called him Dwight; then, six months ago, he'd met Billy. Billy understood what it was like to be one of the new breed, to have been born superior to most men. Billy was superior too, and had a right to call him Dwight. He liked hearing the name again after all this time. It was a key to his psyche, a pleasure button that lifted his spirits each time it was pushed, a reminder that he was destined for a dizzyingly high station in life.

'I tried calling you several times last night,' Billy said.

'I unplugged the phone so I could drink some Scotch and sleep in peace.'

'Have you seen the papers this morning?'

'I just got up.'

'You haven't heard anything about Harris?'

'Who?'

'Graham Harris. The psychic.'

'Oh. No. Nothing. What's to hear?'

'Get the papers, Dwight. And then we'd better have lunch. You are off work today, aren't you?'

'I'm always off Thursdays and Fridays. But what's wrong?'

'The *Daily News* will tell you what's wrong. Be sure to get a copy. We'll have lunch at The Leopard at eleven-thirty.'

Frowning, Bollinger said, 'Look –'

'Eleven-thirty, Dwight.'

Billy hung up.

The day was dreary and cold. Thick dark clouds scudded southward; they were so low they seemed to skim the tops of the highest buildings.

Three blocks from the restaurant, Bollinger left

his taxi and bought the *Daily News* at a kiosk. In his bulky coat and sweaters and gloves and scarves and wool toboggan cap, the vendor looked like a mummy.

The lower half of the front page held a publicity photograph of Edna Mowry provided by the Rhinestone Palace. She was smiling, quite lovely. The upper half of the page featured bold black headlines:

BUTCHER KILLS NUMBER 10
PSYCHIC PREDICTS MURDER

At the corner he turned to the second page and tried to read the story while waiting for the traffic light to change. The wind stung his eyes and made them water. It rattled the paper in his hands and made it impossible for him to read.

He crossed the street and stepped into the sheltered entranceway of an office building. His teeth still chattering from the cold, but free of the wind, he read about Graham Harris and *Manhattan at Midnight*.

His name is Dwight, Harris had said.

The police already know him, Harris had said.

Christ! How could the son of a bitch possibly know so much? Psychic powers? That was a lot of bullshit. There weren't such things. Were there?

Worried now, Bollinger walked to the corner, threw the newspaper into a litter basket, hunched his shoulders against the wind, and hurried toward the restaurant.

The Leopard, on Fiftieth Street near Second Avenue, was a charming restaurant with only a handful of tables and excellent food. The dining area was no larger than an average living room. A hideous display of artificial flowers filled the center of the room, but that was the only really outrageous element in a generally bland decor.

Billy was sitting at a choice table by the window. In an hour The Leopard would be full of diners and noisy conversation. This early, fifteen minutes or more before the executive lunch crowd could slip away from conference rooms and desks, Billy was the only customer. Bollinger sat opposite him. They shook hands and ordered drinks.

'Nasty weather,' Billy said. His Southern accent was heavy.

'Yes.'

They stared at each other over the bud vase and single rose that stood in the center of the table.

'Nasty news,' Billy said at last.

'Yes.'

'What do you think?'

'This Harris is incredible,' Bollinger said.

'Dwight . . . Nobody but me knows you by that name. He hasn't given them much of a clue.'

'My middle name's on all my records – on my employee file at the department.'

Unfolding a linen napkin, Billy said, 'They've got no reason to believe the killer's a policeman.'

'Harris told them they already knew the Butcher.'

'They'll just suppose that he's someone they've already questioned.'

Frowning, Bollinger said, 'If he gives them one more bit of detail, one more clue, I'm blown.'

'I thought you didn't believe in psychics.'

'I was wrong. You were right.'

'Apology accepted,' Billy said, smiling thinly.

'This Harris – can we reason with him?'

'No.'

'He wouldn't understand?'

'He's not one of us.'

The waiter came with their drinks.

When they were alone again, Bollinger said, 'I've never seen this Harris. What does he look like?'

'I'll describe him to you later. Right now . . . do you mind telling me what you're going to do?'

Bollinger didn't have to think about that. Without hesitation he said, 'Kill him.'

'Ah,' Billy said softly.

'Objections?'

'Absolutely none.'

'Good.' Bollinger swallowed half of his drink. 'Because I'd do it even if you had objections.'

The captain came to the table and asked if they would like to hear the menu.

'Give us five minutes,' Billy said. When the captain had gone, he said, 'When you've killed Harris, will you leave him like the Butcher would?'

'Why not?'

'Well, the others have been women.'

'This will confuse and upset them even more.' Bollinger said.

'When will you do it?'

'Tonight.'

Billy said, 'I don't think he lives alone.'

'With his mother?' Bollinger asked sourly.

'No. I believe he lives with a woman.'

'Young?'

'I would imagine so.'

'Pretty?'

'He *does* seem to be a man of good taste.'

'Well, that's just fine,' Bollinger said.

'I thought you'd see it that way.'

'A double-header' Bollinger said. 'That just adds to the fun.' He grinned.

[illegible]

Detective Predusk is rig[illegible]

'I'll talk to him. Put him through[illegible]

'Sorry to bother you [illegible]
formal than we've been [illegible]

'Sure.'

'Please call me Ira.'

'I'd be honored.'

'You're very kind [illegible]
something.'

'No.'

'I know you're a [illegible]
called you back into [illegible]
back at your conven[illegible]

'You didn't interr[illegible]

'You know that was [illegible]
the Mowry apartment[illegible]

'Too clearly.'

'Well, I've been trying to [illegible]
for the past few hours, and [illegible]

'You're still on duty at two in the [illegible]

'No, no. I'm at home.'

'Don't you ever sleep?'

'I wish I could. I haven't been able [illegible]
than four or five hours a day [illegible]

8

Detective Preduski is on the line, Mr Harris.'

'I'll talk to him. Put him through. Hello?'

'Sorry to bother you, Graham. Can we be less formal than we've been? May I call you Graham?'

'Sure.'

'Please call me Ira.'

'I'd be honored.'

'You're very kind. I hope I didn't interrupt something.'

'No.'

'I know you're a busy man. Would you rather I called you back later? Or would you like to call me back at your convenience?'

'You didn't interrupt. What is it you want?'

'You know that writing we found on the walls of the Mowry apartment?'

'Too clearly.'

'Well, I've been trying to track down the source for the past few hours, and –'

'You're still on duty at two in the afternoon?'

'No, no. I'm at home.'

'Don't you ever sleep?'

'I wish I could. I haven't been able to sleep more than four or five hours a day for the past twenty years. I'm probably ruining my health. I *know* I am. But I've got this twisted brain. My head's full of garbage, thousands of useless facts, and I can't stop thinking about them. I keep picking at the damndest things. Like the writing on the walls at the Mowry apartment. I couldn't sleep for thinking about it.'

'And you've come up with something?'

'Well, I told you last night the poetry rang a bell. "Rintah roars and shakes his fires in the burden'd air; Hungry clouds swag on the deep." As soon as I saw it I said to myself, "Ira, that's from something William Blake wrote." You see, when I was in college for that one year, my major was literature. I had to write a paper on Blake. Twenty-five years ago. You see what I mean about garbage in my head? I remember the most useless things. Anyway this morning I bought the Erdman edition of Blake's poetry and prose. Sure enough, I found those lines in "The Argument," part of *The Marriage of Heaven and Hell*. Do you know Blake?'

'I'm afraid not.'

'He was a mystic and a psychic.'

'Clairvoyant?'

'No. But with a psychic bent. He thought men had the power to be gods. For an important part of his career he was a poet of chaos and cataclysm – and yet he was fundamentally a table-pounding optimist. Now, do you remember the line the Butcher printed on the bedroom door?'

'Yes. "A rope over an abyss." '

'Do you have any idea what that's from?'

'None.'

'Neither did I. My head is full of garbage. There's no room for anything important. And I'm not a well-educated man. Not well educated at all. So I called a friend of mine, a professor in the Department of English at Columbia. He didn't recognize the line either, but he passed it around to a few of his colleagues. One of them thought he knew it. He got a concordance of the major philosophers and located the full quotation. "Man is rope stretched between the animal and the Superman - a rope over an abyss." '

'Who said it?'

'Hitler's favorite philosopher.'

'Nietzsche.'

'You know his work?'

'In passing.'

'He believed men could be gods - or at least that certain men could be gods if their society allowed them to grow and exercise their powers. He believed mankind was evolving toward godhood. You see, there's a superficial resemblance between Blake and Nietzsche. That's why the Butcher might quote both of them. But there's a problem, Graham.'

'What's that?'

'Blake was an optimist all the way. Nietzsche was a raving pessimist. Blake thought mankind had a bright future. Nietzsche thought mankind *should* have a bright future, but he believed that it would destroy itself before the Supermen ever evolved from it. Blake apparently liked women. Nietzsche despised them. In fact, he thought women constituted one of the greatest obstacles standing between man and his climb to godhood. You see what I'm getting at?'

'You're saying that if the Butcher subscribes to both Blake and Nietzsche's philosophies, then he's a schizophrenic.'

'Yet you say he's not even crazy.'

'Wait a minute.'

'Last night –'

'All I said was that if he's a maniac, he's a *new kind* of maniac. I said he wasn't crazy in any traditional sense.'

'Which rules out schizophrenia?'

'I guess it does, Ira.'

'But I think it's a good bet . . . maybe I'm wrong . . . God knows . . . but maybe he looks at himself as one of Nietzsche's Supermen. A psychiatrist would call that delusions of grandeur. And delusions of grandeur characterize schizophrenia and paranoia. Do you *still* think the Butcher could pass any psychiatric test we could give him?'

'Yes.'

'You sense this psychically.'

'That's right.'

'Have you ever sensed something and been wrong?'

'Not seriously wrong. No worse than thinking Edna Mowry's name was Edna Dancer.'

'Of course. I know your reputation. I know you're good. I didn't mean to imply anything. You understand? But still – now where do I stand?'

'I don't know.'

'Graham . . . if you were to sit down with a book of Blake's poems, if you were to spend an hour or so reading them, would that maybe put you in tune with the Butcher? Would it spark something – if not a vision, at least a hunch?'

'It might.'

'Would you do me a favor then?'

'Name it.'

'If I send a messenger right over with an edition

of Blake's work, will you sit down with it for an hour and see what happens?'

'You can send it over today if you want, but I won't get to it until tomorrow.'

'Maybe just *half* an hour.'

'Not even that. I've got to finish working on one of my magazines and get it off to the printer tomorrow morning. I'm already three days late with the issue. I'll be working most of tonight. But tomorrow afternoon or evening, I'll make time for Blake.'

'Thank you. I appreciate it. I really do. I'm counting on you. You're my only hope. This Butcher is too much for me, too sharp for me. I'm getting nowhere. Absolutely nowhere. If we don't get a solid lead soon, I don't know what's going to happen.'

[illegible]

Paul Stevenson was wearing [illegible] shirt, a blue-and-black [illegible] sive black suit, black [illegible] with white stitching. [illegible] Prime's office, [illegible] unaware that Prime [illegible] shoes, he was upset [illegible] shouting and screaming [illegible] why are you keeping [illegible]

Prime was stretched [illegible] propped on a [illegible] New York Times, [illegible]

"I just found out [illegible] pany has hired [illegible] on Graham Harris."

"They're not snooping [illegible] is establish Harris's [illegible] on certain days."

"You asked the detectives [illegible] Harris or his girl friend [illegible] And you asked them [illegible] which triples the cost. [illegible] he was, why don't you ask him [illegible]

"I think he'd lie to me [illegible]

9

Paul Stevenson was wearing a hand-sewn blue shirt, a blue-and-black-striped silk tie, an expensive black suit, black socks, and light brown shoes with white stitching. When he came into Anthony Prine's office at two o'clock Friday afternoon, unaware that Prine winced when he saw the shoes, he was upset. Because he was incapable of shouting and screaming at Prine, he pouted. 'Tony, why are you keeping secrets from me?'

Prine was stretched out on the couch, his head propped on a bolster pillow. He was reading *The New York Times*. 'Secrets?'

'I just found out that at your direction the company has hired a private detective agency to snoop on Graham Harris.'

'They're not snooping. All I've asked them to do is establish Harris's whereabouts at certain hours on certain days.'

'You asked the detectives not to approach Harris or his girl friend directly. That's snooping. And you asked them for a forty-eight-hour rush job, which triples the cost. If you want to know where he was, why don't you ask him yourself?'

'I think he'd lie to me.'

'Why should he lie? What certain hours? What certain dates?'

Prine put down the paper, sat up, stood up, stretched. 'I want to know where he was when each of those ten women was killed.'

Perplexed, blinking somewhat stupidly, Stevenson said, 'Why?'

'If on all ten occasions he was alone – working alone, seeing a movie alone, walking alone – then maybe he could have killed them.'

'*Harris*? You think Harris is the Butcher?'

'Maybe.'

'You hire detectives on a maybe?'

'I told you, I've distrusted that man from the start. And if I'm right about this, what a scoop we'll have!'

'But Harris isn't a killer. He *catches* killers.'

Prine went to the bar. 'If a doctor treats fifty patients for influenza one week and fifty more the next, would it surprise you if he got influenza himself during the third week?'

'I'm not sure I get your point.'

Prine filled his glass with bourbon. 'For years Harris has been tuning in to murder with the deepest levels of his mind, exposing himself to trauma as few of us ever do. He has been literally delving into the minds of wife killers, child killers, mass murderers. . . . He's probably seen more blood and violence than most career cops. Isn't it conceivable that a man, unstable to begin with, could crack from all the violent input? Isn't it conceivable that he could become the kind of maniac he's worked so hard to catch?'

'Unstable?' Stevenson frowned. 'Graham Harris is as stable as you or me.'

'How well do you know him?'

'I saw him on the show.'

'There's a bit more you should know.' Prine caught sight of himself in the mirror behind the bar cabinet; he smoothed his lustrous white hair with one hand.

'For example?'

'I'll indulge myself in amateur psychoanalysis – amateur but probably accurate. First of all, Graham Harris was born into border line poverty and –'

'Hold on. His old man was Evan Harris, the publisher.'

'His stepfather. His real father died when Graham was a year old. His mother was a cocktail waitress. She had trouble keeping a roof over their heads because she had to pay off her husband's medical bills. For years they lived day to day, on the edge of disaster. That would leave marks on a child.'

'How did she meet Evan Harris?' Stevenson asked.

'I don't know. But after they were married, Graham took his stepfather's name. He spent the latter part of his childhood in a mansion. After he got his university degree, he had enough time and money to become one of the world's leading climbers. Old man Harris encouraged him. In some circles, Graham was famous, a star. Do you realize how many beautiful women are drawn to the sport of climbing?'

Stevenson shrugged.

'Not as participants,' Prine said. 'As companions to the participants, as bedmates. More women than you'd think. I guess it's the nearness of death that attracts them. For more than a decade,

Graham was adored, made over. Then he took a bad fall. When he recovered, he was terrified of climbing.' Prine was listening to his own voice, fascinated by the theory he had developed. 'Do you understand, Paul? He was born a nobody, lived the first six years of his life as a nobody – then overnight he became a somebody when his mother married Evan Harris. Now is it any wonder that he's afraid of being a nobody again?'

Stevenson went to the bar and poured himself some bourbon. 'It's not likely he'll be a nobody again. He *did* inherit his stepfather's money.'

'Money isn't the same as fame. Once he'd been a celebrity, even within the tight circle of climbing enthusiasts, maybe he developed a habit for it. Maybe he became a fame junkie. It can happen to the best. I've seen it.'

'So have I.'

'If that's what he is . . . well, maybe he's decided that being infamous is as good as being famous. As the Butcher, he's grabbing headlines; he's infamous, even if only under a *nom de guerre*.'

'But he was with you in the studio last night when the Mowry girl was murdered.'

'Maybe not.'

'What? He predicted her death.'

'Did he? Or did he simply tell us who he had selected for his next victim?'

Stevenson stared at him as if he were mad.

Laughing, Prine said, 'Of course Harris was in the studio with me – but perhaps not when the murder took place. I used a source in the police department and got a copy of the coroner's report. According to the pathologist Edna Mowry was murdered sometime between eleven-thirty

Thursday night and one-thirty Friday morning. Now, Graham Harris left the studio at twelve-thirty Friday morning. He had an hour to get to Edna Mowry.'

Stevenson swallowed some bourbon. 'Jesus, Tony, if you're right, if you break a story like this, ABC will give you a late-night talk show and let you do it your way, *live*!'

'They might.'

Stevenson finished his bourbon. 'But you don't have any proof. It's just a theory. And a pretty far-out theory at that. You can't convict a man because he was born to poor parents. Hell, your childhood was worse than his, and you're not a killer.'

'At the moment I've got no proof,' Prine said. But if it can't be found, it can be manufactured, he thought.

Sarah Piper spent the [illegible] noon packing for a five-day [illegible] Nolan, a man's clothing [illegible] been on her special [illegible] years went to see [illegible] with him. He paid [illegible] her time in bed [illegible] gambling stake [illegible] which he was not [illegible] tion for her.

Beginning today, [illegible] the Rhinestone [illegible] hadn't tried to [illegible] before catching the [illegible] morning. She'd [illegible] returning from the [illegible] had been plagued by [illegible] to rest well tonight [illegible] other form for Ramse[illegible]

As she packed, she [illegible] thing missing from her [illegible] She had cried last night [illegible] by Edna's death. But [illegible] again. She was excit[illegible]

10

Sarah Piper spent the early part of Friday afternoon packing for a five-day trip to Las Vegas. Ernie Nolan, a men's clothing manufacturer who had been on her special list of customers for three years, went to Vegas every six months and took her with him. He paid her fifteen hundred dollars for her time in bed and gave her five hundred as a gambling stake. Even if Ernie had been a beast, which he was not, it would have been a good vacation for her.

Beginning today, she was on a week's leave from the Rhinestone Palace; and she was glad that she hadn't tried to squeeze in one more night's work before catching the flight to Vegas tomorrow morning. She'd had only two hours' sleep after returning from Edna's place, and those two hours had been plagued by nightmares. She would need to rest well tonight if she was going to be at the top of her form for Ernie.

As she packed, she wondered if there was something missing from her. Heart? Normal emotions? She had cried last night, had been deeply affected by Edna's death. But already her spirits were high again. She was excited, pleased to be getting away from New York. Introspection didn't give rise to any guilt. She had seen too much of the world – too much violence, desperation, selfishness and grubbiness – to chastise herself for being unable to sustain her grief. That was the way people were built: forgetfulness was the hub of the wheel, the core of the mind, the thing that kept you sane. Maybe that was not pleasant to contemplate, but it was true.

At three o'clock, as she was locking the third suitcase, a man called. He wanted to set up a date for that evening. She didn't know him, but he claimed to have gotten her name from one of her regular clients. Although he sounded quite nice – a genuine Southern gentleman with a mellow accent – she had to turn him down.

'If you've got something else going,' he said, 'I can make it worth your while to drop him for tonight.'

'There's no one else. But I'm going to Vegas in the morning, and I need my rest.'

'What's your usual rate?' he asked.

'Two hundred. But –'

'I'll give you three hundred.'

She hesitated.

'Four hundred.'

'I'll give you the names of a couple of girls –'

'I want to spend the evening with *you*. I hear you're the loveliest woman in Manhattan.'

She laughed. 'You'd be in for a big disappointment.'

'I've made up my mind. When I've made up my mind, nothing on God's earth can change it. Five hundred dollars.'

'That's too much. If you –'

'Young lady, five hundred is peanuts. I've made millions in the oil business. Five hundred - and I won't tie you up all evening. I'll be there around six o'clock. We'll relax together - then go out to dinner. You'll be home by ten, plenty of time to rest up for Vegas.'

'You don't give up easily, do you?'

'That's my trademark. I'm blessed with perseverance. Down home they call it pure mule-headed stubbornness.'

Smiling, she said, 'All right. You win. Five hundred. But you promise we'll be back by ten?'

'Word of honor,' he said.

'You haven't told me your name.'

'Plover', he said. 'Billy James Plover.'

'Do I call you Billy James?'

'Just Billy.'

'Who recommended me?'

'I'd rather not use his name on the phone.'

'Okay. Six o'clock it is.'

'Don't you forget.'

'I'm looking forward to it,' she said.

'So am I,' Billy said.

11

Although Connie Davis had slept late and hadn't opened the antique shop until after lunch, and although she'd had only one customer, it was a good day for business. She had sold six perfectly matched seventeenth-century Spanish chairs. Each piece was of dark oak with bowed legs and claw feet. The arms ended in snarling demon heads, elaborately carved gargoyles the size of oranges. The woman who purchased the chairs had a fourteen-room apartment overlooking Fifth Avenue and Central Park; she wanted them for the room in which she sometimes held séances.

Later, when she was alone in the shop, Connie went to her alcove office at the rear of the main room. She opened a can of fresh coffee, prepared the percolator.

At the front of the room the big windows rattled noisily. Connie looked up from the percolator to see who had come in. No one was there. The windows were trembling from the sudden violence of the winter weather; the wind had picked up and was gusting fiercely.

She sat down at a neatly kept Sheraton desk from the late 1780s and dialed the number of

Graham's private office phone, bypassing his secretary. When he answered she said, 'Hello, Nick.'

'Hi, Nora.'

'If you've made any headway with your work, let me take you to dinner tonight. I just sold the Spanish chairs, and I feel a need to celebrate.'

'Can't do, I'm afraid. I'm going to have to work most of the night to finish here.'

'Can't the staff work a bit of overtime?' she asked.

'They've done their job. But you know how I am. I have to double-check and triple-check everything.'

'I'll come help.'

'There's nothing you can help with.'

'Then I'll sit in the corner and read.'

'Really, Connie, you'd be bored. You go home and relax. I'll show up sometime around one or two in the morning.'

'Nothing doing. I won't get in your way, and I'll be perfectly comfortable reading in an office chair. Nora needs her Nick tonight. I'll bring supper.'

'Well . . . okay. Who am I kidding? I knew you'd come.'

'A large pizza and a bottle of wine. How's that?'

'Sounds good.'

'When?' she asked.

'I've been dozing over my typewriter. If I'm to get this work done tonight, I'd better take a nap. As soon as the staff clears out for the day, I'll lie down. Why don't you bring the pizza at seven-thirty?'

'Count on it.'

'We'll have company at eight-thirty.'

'Who?'

'A police detective. He wants to discuss some new evidence in the Butcher case.'

'Preduski?' she asked.

'No. One of Preduski's lieutenants. A guy named Bollinger. He called a few minutes ago and wanted to come to the house this evening. I told him that you and I would be working here until late.'

'Well, at least he's coming after we eat,' she said. 'Talking about the Butcher *before* dinner would spoil my appetite.'

'See you at seven-thirty.'

'Sleep tight, Nicky.'

When the percolator shut off, she poured steaming coffee into a mug, added cream, went to the front of the store and sat in a chair near one of the mullioned show windows. She could look over and between the antiques for a many-paned view of a windswept section of Tenth Street.

A few people hurried past, dressed in heavy coats, their hands in their pockets, heads tucked down.

Scattered snowflakes followed the air currents down between the buildings and ricocheted along the pavement.

She sipped her coffee and almost purred as the warmth spread through her.

She thought about Graham and felt warmer still. Nothing could chill her when Graham was on her mind. Not wind. Not snow. Not the Butcher. She felt safe with Graham - even with just the thought of him. Safe and protected. She knew that, in spite of the fear that had grown in him since his fall, he would lay down his life for her if that was ever required of him. Just as she would give her life to save his. It wasn't likely that either of them would be presented with such a dramatic choice; but she was convinced that Graham would find his courage gradually in the weeks and months ahead, would find it without the help of a crisis.

Suddenly the wind exploded against the window, howled and moaned and pasted snow, like specks of froth and spittle, to the cold glass.

12

The room was long and narrow with a brown tile floor, beige walls, a high ceiling and fluorescent lights. Two metal desks stood just inside the door; they held typewriters, letter trays, vases full of artificial flowers, and the detritus of a day's work. The two well-dressed matronly women behind the desks were cheerful in spite of the drab institutional atmosphere. There were five cafeteria tables lined up, short end to short end, so that whoever sat at them would always be sideways to the desks. The ten metal chairs were all on the same side of the table row. Except for the relationship of the tables to the desks, it might have been a schoolroom, a study hall monitored by two teachers.

Frank Bollinger identified himself as Ben Frank and said he was an employee of a major New York City firm of architects. He asked for the complete file on the Bowerton Building, took off his coat and sat at the first table.

The two women, as efficient as they appeared to be, quickly brought him the Bowerton material from an adjacent storage room: original blueprints, amendments to the blueprints, cost estimates, applications for dozens of different building permits, final cost sheets, remodeling plans, photographs, letters ... Every form - and everything else required by law - that was related to the Bowerton highrise and that had passed officially through a city bureau or department was in that file. It was a formidable mound of paper, even though each piece was carefully labeled and both categorically and sequentially arranged.

The forty-two-story Bowerton Building, facing a busy block of Lexington Avenue, had been completed in 1929 and stood essentially unchanged. It was one of Manhattan's art deco masterpieces, even more effectively designed than the justly acclaimed art deco Chanin Building which was only a few blocks away. More than a year ago a group of concerned citizens had launched a campaign to have the building declared a landmark in order to keep its most spectacular art deco features from being wiped away during sporadic flurries of 'modernization.' But the most important fact, so far as Bollinger was concerned, was that Graham Harris had his offices on the fortieth floor of the Bowerton Building.

For an hour and ten minutes, Bollinger studied the paper image of the structure. Main entrances. Service entrances. One-way emergency exits. The placement and operation of the bank of sixteen elevators. The placement of the two stairwells. A minimal electronic security system, primarily a closed-circuit television guard station, had been installed in 1969; and he went over and over the paper on that until he was certain that he had overlooked no detail of it.

At four forty-five he stood up, yawned and

stretched. Smiling, humming softly, he put on his overcoat.

Two blocks from City Hall he stepped into a telephone booth and called Billy. 'I've checked it out.'

'Bowerton?'

'Yeah.'

'What do you think?' 'Billy asked anxiously.

'It can be done.'

'My God. You're sure?'

'As sure as I can be until I start it.'

'Maybe I should be more help. I could –

'No,' Bollinger said. 'If anything goes wrong, I can flash my badge and say I showed up to investigate a complaint. Then I can slip quietly away. But if we were both there, how could we explain our way out of it?'

'I suppose you're right.'

'We'll stick to the original plan.'

'All right.'

'You be in that alleyway at ten o'clock.'

Billy said, 'What if you get there and discover it won't work? I don't want to be waiting –'

'If I have to give it up,' Bollinger said, 'I'll call you well before ten. But if you don't get the call, *be in that alley*.'

'Of course. What else? But I won't wait past ten-thirty. I *can't* wait longer than that.'

'That'll be long enough.'

Billy sighed happily. 'Are we going to stand this city on its ear?'

'Nobody will sleep tomorrow night.'

'Have you decided what lines you'll write on the wall?'

Bollinger waited until a city bus rumbled past

the booth. His choice of quotations was clever; and he wanted Billy to appreciate them. 'Yeah. I've got a long one from Nietzsche. "I want to teach men the sense of their existence, which is Superman, the lightning out of the dark cloud man." '

'Oh, that's excellent,' Billy said. 'I couldn't have chosen better myself.'

'Thank you.'

'And Blake?'

'Just a fragment from the alternate seventh night of *The Four Zoas*. "Hearts laid open to the light . . ." '

Billy laughed.

'I knew you'd like it.'

'I suppose you *do* intend to lay their hearts open?'

'Naturally,' Bollinger said. 'Their hearts and everything else, from throat to crotch.'

13

Promptly at six o'clock, the doorbell rang.

Sarah Piper answered it. Her professional smile slipped when she saw who was standing in the hall. 'What are *you* doing here?' she asked, surprised.

'May I come in?'

'Well . . .'

'You look beautiful tonight. Absolutely stunning.'

She was wearing a tight burnt-orange pantsuit, flimsy, with a low neckline that revealed too much of her creamy breasts. Self-consciously she put one hand over her cleavage. 'I'm sorry, but I can't ask you in. I'm expecting someone.'

'You're expecting me,' he said. 'Billy James Plover.'

'What? That's not your name.'

'It surely is. It's the name I was born with. I changed it years ago, of course.'

'Why didn't you give me your real name on the phone?'

'I've got to protect my reputation.'

Still confused, she stepped back to let him pass. She closed the door and locked it. Aware that she was being rude but unable to control herself, she stared openly at him. She couldn't think what to say.

'You seem shocked, Sarah.'

'Yeah,' she said. 'I guess I am. It's just that you don't seem like the sort of man who would come to a woman – to someone like me.'

He had been smiling from the moment she'd opened the door. Now his face broke into a broad grin. 'What's wrong with someone like you? You're gorgeous.'

This is crazy, she thought.

She said, 'Your voice.'

'The Southern accent?'

'Yeah.'

'That's also part of my youth, just like the name. Would you prefer I dropped it?'

'Yeah. Your talking like that – it's not right. It's creepy.' She hugged herself.

'Creepy? I thought you'd be amused. And when I'm Billy . . . I don't know . . . I kind of have fun with it . . . kind of feel like someone altogether new.' He stared hard at her and said, 'Something's wrong. We're off on the wrong foot. Or maybe worse than that. Is it worse than that? If you don't want to go to bed with me, say so. I'll understand. Maybe something about me repels you. I haven't always been successful with women. I've lost out many times. God knows. So just tell me. I'll leave. No hard feelings.'

She put on her professional smile again and shook her head. Her thick blond hair bounced prettily. 'I'm sorry. There's no need for you to go. I was just surprised, that's all.'

'You're sure?'

'Positive.'

He looked at the living room beyond the foyer arch, reached down to finger the antique umbrella stand beside the door. 'You have a nice place.'

'Thank you.' She opened the foyer closet, plucked a hanger from the clothes rod. 'Let me take your coat.'

He took it off, handed it to her.

As she put the coat in the closet, she said, 'Your gloves too. I'll put them in a coat pocket.'

'I'll keep my gloves,' he said.

When she turned back to him, he was standing between her and the front door, and he was holding a wicked switchblade knife in his right hand.

She said, 'Put that away.'

'What did you say?'

'*Put that away!*'

He laughed.

'I mean it,' she said.

'You're the coolest bitch I've ever met.'

'Put that knife in your pockot. Put it away and then get out of here.'

Waving the knife at her, he said, 'When they realize I'm going to slit them open, they say some silly things. But I don't believe any of them ever *seriously* thought she could talk me out of it. Until you. So very cool.'

She twisted away from him. She ran out of the foyer, into the living room. Her heart was pounding; she was shaking badly; but she was determined not to be incapacitated by fear. She kept a gun in the top drawer of her nightstand. If she could get into the bedroom, close and lock the door between them, she could hold him off long enough to put her hands on the pistol.

Within a few steps he caught her by the shoulder. She tried to jerk free.

He was stronger than he looked. His fingers

were like talons. He swung her around and shoved her backward.

Off balance, she collided with the coffee table, fell over it. She struck her hip on one of the heavy wooden legs; pain like an incandescent bulb flashed along her thigh.

He stood over her, still holding the knife, still grinning.

'Bastard,' she said.

'There are two ways you can die, Sarah. You can try to run and resist, forcing me to kill you now – painfully and slowly. Or you can cooperate, come into the bedroom, let me give you some fun. Then I promise you'll die quickly and painlessly.'

Don't panic, she told herself. You're Sarah Piper, and you came out of nothing, and you made something of yourself, and you have been knocked down dozens of times before, knocked down figuratively and literally, and you've always gotten up, and you'll get up this time, and you'll survive, you will, dammit, you will.

'Okay,' she said. She stood up.

'Good girl.' He held the knife out at his side. He unbuttoned the bodice of her pantsuit and slipped his free hand under the thin material. 'Nice,' he said.

She closed her eyes as he moved nearer.

'I'll make it fun for you,' he said.

She drove her knee into his crotch.

Although the blow didn't land squarely, he staggered backward.

She grabbed a table lamp and threw it. Without waiting to see if it hit him, she ran into the bedroom and shut the door.

Before she could lock it, he slammed against the

far side and pushed the door open two or three inches.

She tried to force it shut again so that she could throw the lock, but he was stronger than she. She knew she couldn't hold out against him for more than a minute or two. Therefore, when he was pressing the hardest and would expect it the least, she let go of the door altogether and ran to the nightstand.

Surprised, he stumbled into the room and nearly fell.

She pulled open the nightstand drawer and picked up the gun.

He knocked it out of her hand. It clattered against the wall and dropped to the floor, out of reach.

Why didn't you scream? she asked herself. Why didn't you yell for help while you could hold the door shut? It's unlikely anyone would hear you in soundly built apartments like these, but at least it was worth a try when you had a chance.

But she knew why she didn't cry out. She was Sarah Piper. She had never called for help in her life. She had always solved her own problems, had always fought her own battles. She was tough and proud of it. She did not scream.

She was terrified, trembling, sick with fear, but she knew that she had to die the same way she had lived. If she broke now, whimpered and mewled when there wasn't any chance of salvation, she would be making a lie of her life. If her life was to have meant anything, anything at all, she would have to die as she had lived: resolute, proud, tough.

She spat in his face.

14

'Homicide.'

'I want to speak to a detective.'

'What's his name?'

'Any detective. I don't care.'

'Is this an emergency?'

'Yes.'

'Where are you calling from?'

'Never mind. I want a detective.'

'I'm required to take your address, telephone number, name –'

'Stuff it! Let me talk to a detective or I'll hang up.'

'Detective Martin speaking.'

'I just killed a woman.'

'Where are you calling from?'

'Her apartment.'

'What's the address?'

'She was very beautiful.'

'What's the address?'

'A lovely girl.'

'What was her name?'

'Sarah.'

'Do you know her last name?'

'Piper.'

'Will you spell that?'

'P-i-p-e-r.'

'Sarah Piper.'

'That's right.'

'What's your name?'

'The Butcher.'

'What's your real name?'

'I'm not going to tell you.'

'Yes, you are. That's why you called.'

'No. I called to tell you I'm going to kill some more people before the night's out.'

'Who?'

'One of them is the woman I love.'

'What's her name?'

'I wish I didn't have to kill her.'

'Then don't. You –'

'But I think she suspects.'

'Why don't we –'

'Nietzsche was right.'

'Who?'

'Nietzsche.'

'Who's he?'

'A philosopher.'

'Oh.'

'He was right about women.'

'What did he say about women?'

'They just get in our way. They hold us back from perfection. All those energies we put into courting them and screwing them – wasted! All that wasted sex energy could be put to other use, to thought and study. If we didn't waste our energies on women, we could evolve into what we were meant to be.'

'And what were we meant to be?'

'Are you trying to trace this call?'

'No, no.'

'Yes. Of course you are.'

'No, really we aren't.'

'I'll be gone from here in a minute. I just wanted to tell you that tomorrow you'll know who I am, who the Butcher is. But you won't catch me. I'm the lightning out of the dark cloud man.'

'Let's try to –'

'Good-bye, Detective Martin.'

[illegible]

At seven o'clock Friday evening, [illegible] began to fall in Manhattan [illegible] a full-scale storm. The [illegible] sky and made pale, [illegible] streets.

In his living room, [illegible] millions of tiny flakes [illegible] The snow pleased him [illegible] ahead, and now, especially [illegible] weather, it was [illegible] Harris and his wom[illegible] Coventry Building [illegible] getting to them [illegible] hitch had improved [illegible] an accomplice.

At seven-twenty, [illegible] hall closet, slipped into [illegible]

The pistol was already [illegible] He wasn't using his police [illegible] lets from that could be traced [illegible] Walther PPK, a compact [illegible] from importation into the United States [illegible] A slightly larger pistol, the [illegible] now manufactured for [illegible]

15

At seven o'clock Friday evening, a fine dry snow began to fall in Manhattan, not merely flurries but a full-scale storm. The snow sifted out of the black sky and made pale, shifting patterns on the dark streets.

In his living room, Frank Bollinger watched the millions of tiny flakes streaming past the window. The snow pleased him no end. With the weekend ahead, and now especially with the change of weather, it was doubtful that anyone other than Harris and his woman would be working late in the Bowerton Building. He felt that his chances of getting to them and pulling off the plan without a hitch had improved considerably. The snow was an accomplice.

At seven-twenty, he took his overcoat from the hall closet, slipped into it and buttoned up.

The pistol was already in the right coat pocket. He wasn't using his police revolver, because bullets from that could be traced too easily. This was a Walther PPK, a compact .38 that had been banned from importation into the United States since 1969. (A slightly larger pistol, the Walther PPK/S, was now manufactured for marketing in the United

States; it was less easily concealed than the original model). There was a silencer on the piece, not homemade junk but a precision-machined silencer made by Walther for use by various elite European police agencies. Even with the silencer screwed in place, the gun fit easily out of sight in the deep overcoat pocket. Bollinger had taken the weapon off a dead man, a suspect in a narcotics and prostitution investigation. The moment he saw it he knew that he must have it; and he failed to report finding it as he should have done. That was nearly a year ago; he'd had no occasion to use it until tonight.

In his left coat pocket, Bollinger was carrying a box of fifty bullets. He didn't think he'd need more than were already in the pistol's magazine, but he intended to be prepared for any eventuality.

He left the apartment and took the stairs two at a time, eager for the hunt to begin.

Outside, the grainy, wind-driven snow was like bits of ground glass. The night howled spectrally between the buildings and rattled the branches of the trees.

Graham Harris's office, the largest of the five rooms in the Harris Publications suite on the fortieth floor of the Bowerton Building, didn't look like a place where business was transacted. It was paneled in dark wood - real and solid wood, not veneer - and had a textured beige acoustical ceiling. The forest-green ceiling-to-floor drapes matched the plush carpet. The desk had once been a Steinway piano; the guts had been ripped out, the lid lowered and cut to fit the frame. Behind the desk rose bookshelves filled with volumes about skiing and climbing. The light came from four floor-lamps with old-fashioned ceramic sconces and glass chimneys that hid the electric bulbs. There were also two brass reading lamps on the desk. A small conference table and four armchairs occupied the space in front of the windows. A richly carved seventeenth-century British coatrack stood by the door to the corridor, and an antique bar of cut glass, beveled mirrors and inlaid woods stood by the door to the reception lounge. On the walls were photographs of climbing teams in action, and there was one oil painting, a mountain snowscape. The room might have been a study in the home of a retired professor, where books were read and pipes were smoked and where a spaniel lay curled at the feet of its master.

Connie opened the foil-lined box on the conference table. Steam rose from the pizza; a spicy aroma filled the office.

The wine was chilled. In the pizzeria, she had made them keep the bottle in their refrigerator until the pie was ready to go.

Famished, they ate and drank in silence for a few minutes.

Finally she said, 'Did you take a nap?'

'Did I ever.'

'How long?'

'Two hours.'

'Sleep well?'

'Like the dead.'

'You don't look it.'

'Dead?'

'You don't look like you'd slept.'

'Maybe I dreamed it.'

'You've got dark rings under your eyes.'

'My Rudolph Valentino look.'

'You should go home to bed.'

'And have the printer down my throat tomorrow?'

'They're *quarterly* magazines. A few days one way or the other won't matter.'

'You're talking to a perfectionist.'

'Don't I know it.'

'A perfectionist who loves you.'

She blew him a kiss.

Frank Bollinger parked his car on a side street and walked the last three blocks to the Bowerton Building.

A skin of snow, no more than a quarter inch but growing deeper, sheathed the sidewalks and street. Except for a few taxicabs that spun past too fast for road conditions, there was not much traffic on Lexington Avenue.

The main entrance to the Bowerton Building was set back twenty feet from the sidewalk. There were four revolving glass doors, three of them locked at this hour. Beyond the doors the large lobby rich with marble and brasswork and copper trim, was overflowing with warm amber light.

Bollinger patted the pistol in his pocket and went inside.

Overhead, a closed-circuit television camera was suspended from a brace. It was focused on the only unlocked door.

Bollinger stamped his feet to knock the snow from his shoes and to give the camera time to study him. The man in the control room wouldn't find him suspicious if he faced the camera without concern.

A uniformed security guard was sitting on a stool behind a lectern near the first bank of elevators.

Bollinger walked over to him, stepped out of the camera's range.

'Evening,' the guard said.

As he walked, he took his wallet from an inside pocket and flashed the gold badge. 'Police.' His voice echoed eerily off the marble walls and the high ceiling.

'Something wrong?' the guard asked.

'Anybody working late tonight?'

'Just four.'

'All in the same office?'

'No. What's up?'

Bollinger pointed to the open registry on the lectern. 'I'd like all four names.'

'Let's see here . . . Harris, Davis, Ott and MacDonald.'

'Where would I find Ott?'

'Sixteenth floor.'

'What's the name of the office?'

'Cragmont Imports.'

The guard's face was round and white. He had a weak mouth and a tiny Oliver Hardy mustache. When he tried for an expression of curiosity, the mustache nearly disappeared up his nostrils.

'What floor for MacDonald?' Bollinger asked.

'Same. Sixteenth.'

'He's working with Ott?'

'That's right.'

'Just those four?'

'Just those four.'

'Maybe someone else is working late, and you don't know it.'

'Impossible. After five-thirty, anyone going upstairs has to sign in with me. At six o'clock we go through every floor to see who's working late, and then they check out with us when they leave. 'The building management has set down strict fire-prevention rules. This is part of them.' He patted the registry. 'If there's ever a fire, we'll know exactly who's in the building and where we can find them.'

'What about maintenance crews?'

'What about them?'

'Janitors. Cleaning women. Any working now?'

'Not on Friday night.'

'You're sure?'

'Sure I'm sure.' He was visibly upset by the interrogation and beginning to wonder if he should cooperate. 'They come in all day tomorrow.'

'Building engineer?'

'Schiller. He's night engineer.'

'Where is Schiller?'

'Downstairs.'

'Where downstairs?'

'Checking one of the heat pumps, I think.'

'Is he alone?'

'Yeah.'

'How many other security guards?'

'Are you going to tell me what's up?'

'For God's sake, this is an emergency!' Bollinger said. 'How many security guards besides you?'

'Just two. What emergency?'

'There's been a bomb threat.'

The guard's lips trembled. The mustache seemed about to fall off. 'You're kidding.'

'I wish I were.'

The guard slid off his stool, stepped from behind the lectern.

At the same time Bollinger took the Walther from his pocket.

The guard blanched. 'What's that?'

'A gun. Don't go for yours.'

'Look, this bomb threat . . . *I* didn't call it in.'

Bollinger laughed.

'It's true.'

'I'm sure it is.'

'Hey . . . that gun has a silencer on it.'

'Yeah.'

'But policemen don't –'

Bollinger shot him twice in the chest.

The impact of the bullets threw the guard into the sheet marble. For an instant he stood very straight, as if he were waiting for someone to measure his height and mark it on the wall. Then he collapsed.

Part two

FRIDAY

8:00–8:30 P.M.

16

Bollinger turned immediately from the dead man and looked at the revolving doors. Nobody was there, no one on the sidewalk beyond, no one who might have seen the killing.

Moving quickly but calmly, he tucked the pistol into his pocket and grabbed the body by the arms. He dragged it into the waiting area between the first two banks of elevators. Now, anyone coming to the doors would see only an empty lobby.

The dead man stared at him. The mustache seemed to have been painted on his lip.

Bollinger turned out the guard's pockets. He found quarters, dimes, a crumpled five-dollar bill, and a key ring with seven keys.

He returned to the main part of the lobby.

He wanted to go straight to the door, but he knew that was not a good idea. That would put him in camera range. If the men monitoring the closed-circuit system saw him locking the door, they would be curious. They'd come to investigate, and he would lose the advantage of surprise.

Keeping in mind the details of the plans he had studied at City Hall that afternoon, he walked quietly to the rear of the lobby and stepped into a short corridor on the left. Four rooms led off the hall. The second on the right was the guards' room, and the door was open.

Wondering if the squeaking of his wet shoes sounded as loud to the guards as it did to him, he edged up to the open door.

Inside, two men were talking laconically about their jobs, complaining, but only half-heartedly.

Bollinger took the pistol from his coat pocket. He walked through the doorway.

The men were sitting at a small table in front of three television screens. They weren't watching the monitors. They were playing two-handed pinochle.

The older of the two was in his fifties. Heavy. Gray-haired. He had a prizefighter's lumpy face. The name 'Neely' was stitched on his left shirt pocket. He was slow. He looked up at Bollinger, failed to react as he should have to the gun, and said without fear, 'What's this?'

The other guard was in his thirties. Trim. Ascetic face. Pale hands. As he turned to see what had caught Neely's attention, Bollinger saw 'Faulkner' stitched on his shirt.

He shot Faulkner first.

Reaching with both hands for his ruined throat, too late to stop the life from gushing out of him, Faulkner toppled backward in his chair.

'Hey!' Fat Neely was finally on his feet. His holster was snapped shut. He grappled with it.

Bollinger shot him twice.

Neely did an ungraceful pirouette, fell on the table, collapsed it, and went to the floor in a flutter of pinochle cards.

Bollinger checked their pulses.

They were dead.

When he left the room, he closed the door.

At the front of the big lobby, he locked the last revolving door and put the keys into his pocket.

He went to the lectern, sat on the stool. He took the box of bullets from his left coat pocket and replenished the pistol's magazine.

He looked at his watch. 8:10. He was right on schedule.

17

'That was good pizza,' Graham said.

'Good wine, too. Have another glass.'

'I've had enough.'

'Just a little one.'

'No. I've got to work.'

'Dammit.'

'You knew that when you came.'

'I was trying to get you drunk.'

'On one bottle of wine?'

'And then seduce you.'

'Tomorrow night,' he said.

'I'll be blind with desire by then.'

'Doesn't matter. Love is a Braille experience.'

She winced.

He got up, came around the table, kissed her cheek. 'Did you bring a book to read?'

'A Nero Wolfe mystery.'

'Then read.'

'Can I look at you from time to time?'

'What's to look at?'

'Why do *men* buy *Playboy* magazine?' she asked.

'I won't be working in the nude.'

'You don't have to be.'

'Pretty dull.'

'You're even sexy with your clothes on.'
'Okay,' he said, smiling. 'Look but don't talk.'
'Can I drool?'
'Drool if you must.'
He was pleased with the flattery, and she was delighted by his reaction. She felt that she was gradually chipping away at his inferiority complex, peeling it layer by layer.

18

The building engineer for the night shift was a stocky, fair-skinned blond in his late forties. He was wearing gray slacks and a gray-white-blue checkered shirt. He was smoking a pipe.

When Bollinger came down the steps from the lobby corridor, the gun in his right hand, the engineer said, 'Who the hell are you?' He spoke with a slight German accent.

'*Sie sind Herr Schiller, nicht wahr?*' Bollinger asked. His grandfather and grandmother had been German-Americans; he had learned the language when he was young and had never forgotten it.

Surprised to hear German spoken, worried about the gun but confused by Bollinger's smile, Schiller said. '*Ja, ich bin's.*'

'*Es freut mich sehr Sie kennenzulernen.*'

Schiller took the pipe from his mouth. He licked his lips nervously. '*Die Pistole?*'

'*Fur den Mord,*' Bollinger said. He squeezed off two shots.

Upstairs, on the lobby floor, Bollinger opened the door directly across the hall from the guards' room. He switched on the lights.

The narrow room was lined with telephone and power company equipment. The ceiling and walls were unfinished concrete. Two bright red fire extinguishers were hung where they could be reached quickly.

He went to the far side of the room, to a pair of yard-square metal cabinets that were fixed to the wall. The lid of each cabinet bore the insignia of the telephone company. Although the destruction of the contents would render useless all other routing boxes, switchboards and backup systems, neither of the cabinets was locked. Each housed twenty-six small levers, circuit breakers in a fuse box. They were all inclined toward the 'on' mark. Bollinger switched them off, one by one.

He moved to a box labeled 'Fire Emergency,' forced it open, and tinkered with the wires inside.

That done, he went to the guards' room across the hall. He stepped around the bodies and picked up one of the two telephones that stood in front of the closed-circuit television screens.

No dial tone.

He jiggled the cut-off spikes.

Still no dial tone.

He hung up, picked up the other phone: another dead line.

Whistling softly, Bollinger entered the first elevator.

There were two keyholes in the control panel. The top one opened the panel for repairs. The one at the bottom shut down the lift mechanism.

He tried the keys that he had taken from the dead guard. The third one fit the bottom lock.

He pushed the button for the fifth floor. The number didn't light; the doors didn't close; the elevator didn't move.

Whistling louder than before, he proceeded to shut down fourteen of the remaining fifteen elevators. He would use the last one to go to the sixteenth floor, where Ott and MacDonald were working, and later to the fortieth floor, where Harris and his woman were waiting.

19

Although Graham hadn't spoken, Connie knew that something was wrong. He was breathing heavily. She looked up from her book and saw that he had stopped working and was staring at empty air, his mouth slightly open, his eyes sort of glazed. 'What's the matter?'

'Nothing.'

'You're pale.'

'Just a headache.'

'You're shaking.'

He said nothing.

She got up, put down her book, went to him. She sat on the corner of his desk. 'Graham?'

'It's okay. I'm fine now.'

'No, you aren't.'

'I'm fine.'

'There for a minute you weren't.'

'For a minute I wasn't,' he agreed.

She took his hand; it was icy. 'A vision?'

'Yeah,' Graham said.

'Of what?'

'Me. Getting shot.'

'That's not the least bit funny.'

'I'm not joking.'

'You've never had a *personal* vision before. You've always said the clairvoyance works only when other people are involved.'

'Not this time.'

'Maybe you're wrong.'

'I doubt it. I felt as if I had been hit between the shoulders with a sledgehammer. The wind was knocked out of me. I saw myself falling.' His blue eyes grew wide. 'There was blood. A great deal of blood.'

She felt sick in her soul, in her heart. He had never been wrong, and now he was predicting he would be shot.

He squeezed her hand tightly, as if he were trying to press strength from her into him.

'Do you mean shot - and killed?'

'I don't know,' he said. 'Maybe killed or maybe just wounded. Shot in the back. That much is clear.'

'Who did it - will do it?'

'The Butcher, I think.'

'You saw him?'

'No. Just a strong impression.'

'Where did it happen?'

'Someplace I know well.'

'Here?'

'Maybe . . .'

'At home?'

'Maybe.'

A fierce gust of wind boomed along the side of the highrise. The office windows vibrated behind the drapes.

'When will it happen?' she asked.

'Soon.'

'Tonight?'

'I can't be sure.'

'Tomorrow?'

'Possibly.'

'Sunday?

'Not as late as that.'

'What are we going to do?'

20

The lift stopped at the sixteenth floor.

Bollinger used the key to shut off the elevator before he stepped out of it. The cab would remain where it was, doors open, until he needed it again.

For the most part, the sixteenth floor was shrouded in darkness. An overhead fluorescent tube brightened the elevator alcove, but the only light in the corridor came from two dim red emergency exit bulbs, one at each end of the building.

Bollinger had anticipated the darkness. He took a pencil flashlight from an inside coat pocket, flicked it on.

Ten small businesses maintained offices on the sixteenth floor, six to the right and four to the left of the elevators. He went to the right. Two suites down the hall he found a door that bore the words CRAGMONT IMPORTS.

He turned off the flashlight and put it away.

He took out the Walther PPK.

Christ, he thought, it's going so smoothly. So easily. As soon as he finished at Cragmont Imports, he could go after the primary targets. Harris first. Then the woman. If she was good-looking . . . well, he was so far ahead of schedule now that he had an hour to spare. An hour for the woman if she rated it. He was ready for a woman, full of energy and appetite and excitement. A woman, a table filled with good food, and a lot of fine whiskey. But mostly a woman. In an hour he could use her up, really use her up.

He tried the door to Cragmont Imports. It wasn't locked.

He walked into the reception lounge. The room was gloomy. The only light came from an adjacent office where the door was standing halfway open.

He went to the shaft of light, stood in it, listened to the men talking in the inner office. At last he pushed open the door and went inside.

They were sitting at a conference table that was piled high with papers and bound folders. They weren't wearing their suit jackets or their ties, and their shirt sleeves were rolled up; one was wearing a blue shirt, the other a white shirt. They saw the pistol at once, but they needed several seconds to adjust before they could raise their eyes to look at his face.

'This place smells like perfume.' Bollinger said.

They stared at him.

'Is one of you wearing perfume?'

'No,' said blue shirt. 'Perfume's one of the things we import.'

'Is one of you MacDonald?'

They looked at the gun, at each other, then at the gun again.

'MacDonald?' Bollinger asked.

The one in the blue shirt said, 'He's MacDonald.'

The one in the white shirt said, '*He's* MacDonald.'

'That's a lie,' said the one in the blue shirt.

'No, *he's* lying,' said the other.

'I don't know what you want with MacDonald,' said the one in the blue shirt. 'Just leave me out of it. Do what you have to do to him and go away.'

'Christ almighty!' said the one in the white shirt. 'I'm *not* MacDonald! You want *him*, that son of a bitch there, not me!'

Bollinger laughed. 'It doesn't matter. I'm also here to get Mr Ott.'

'*Me?*' said the one in the blue shirt. 'Who in the hell would want *me* killed?'

21

Connie said, 'You'll have to call Preduski.'

'Why?'

'To get police protection.'

'It's no use.'

'He believes in your visions.'

'I know he does.'

'He'll give you protection.'

'Of course,' Graham said. 'But that's not what I meant.'

'Explain.'

'Connie, I've seen myself shot in the back. It's going to happen. Things I see *always* happen. Nobody can do anything to stop this.'

'There's no such thing as predestination. The future can be changed.'

'Can it?'

'You know it can.'

A haunted look filled his bright blue eyes. 'I doubt that very much.'

'You can't be sure.'

'But I am sure.'

This attitude of his, this willingness to ascribe all of his failings to predestination, worried and upset her more than anything else about him. It was an especially pernicious form of cowardice. He was rejecting all responsibility for his own life.

'Call Preduski,' she said.

He lowered his eyes and stared at her hand but didn't seem to see how tightly he was gripping it.

She said, 'If this man comes to the *house* to kill you, I'll probably be there too. Do you think he's going to shoot you, then just walk away and let *me* live?'

Shocked, as she had known he would be, by the thought of her under the Butcher's knife, he said, 'My God.'

'Call Preduski.'

'All right.' He let go of her hand. He picked up the receiver, listened for a moment, played with the dial, jiggled the buttons.

'What's wrong?'

Frowning, he said, 'No dial tone.' He hung up, waited a few seconds, picked up the receiver again. 'Still nothing.'

She slid off the desk. 'Let's try your secretary's phone.'

They went out to the reception room.

That phone was dead too.

'Funny,' he said.

Her heartbeat quickening, she said, 'Is he going to come after you tonight?'

'I told you, I don't know for sure.'

'Is he in the building right now?'

'You think he cut the telephone line.'

She nodded.

'That's pretty farfetched,' he said. 'It's just a breakdown in service.'

She went to the door, opened it, stepped into the hall. He came behind her, favoring his injured leg.

Darkness lay on most of the corridor. Dim red emergency lights shone at each end of the hall, above the doors to the staircases. Fifty feet away a pool of wan blue light marked the elevator alcove.

Except for the sound of their breathing, the fortieth floor was silent.

'I'm not a clairvoyant,' she said, 'but I don't like the way it feels. I sense it, Graham. Something's wrong.'

'In a building like this, the telephone lines are in the walls. Outside of the building they're underground. All the lines are underground in this city. How would he get to them?'

'I don't know. But maybe *he* knows.'

'He'd be taking such a risk,' Graham said.

'He's taken risks before. Ten times before.'

'But not like this. We're not alone. The security guards are in the building.'

'They're forty stories below.'

'A long way,' he agreed. 'Let's get out of here.'

'We're probably being silly.'

'Probably.'

'We're probably safe where we are.'

'Probably.'

'I'll grab our coats.'

'Forget the coats.' He took hold of her hand. 'Come on. Let's get to those elevators.'

Bollinger needed eight shots to finish off MacDonald and Ott. They kept ducking behind the furniture.

By the time he had killed them, the Walther PPK was no longer firing silently. No silencer could function at peak efficiency for more than a dozen shots; the baffles and wadding were compacted by the bullets, and sound escaped. The last three shots were like the sharp barks of a medium-sized guard dog. But that didn't matter. The noise wouldn't carry to the street or up to the fortieth floor.

In the outer office of Cragmont Imports, he switched on a light. He sat on a couch, reloaded the Walther's magazine, unscrewed the silencer and put it into his pocket. He didn't want to risk fouling the barrel with loose steel fibers from the silencer; besides, there was no one left in the building to hear shots when he killed Harris and the woman. And a shot fired on the fortieth floor would not penetrate walls and windows and travel all the way down to Lexington Avenue.

He looked at his watch. 8:25.

He turned off the light, left Cragmont Imports, and went down the hall to the elevator.

Eight elevators served the fortieth floor, but none of them was working.

Connie pushed the call button on the last lift. When nothing happened, she said, 'The telephone, and now this.'

In the spare yet harsh fluorescent light, Graham's laugh lines looked deeper and sharper than usual; his face resembled that of a kabuki actor painted to represent extreme anxiety. 'We're trapped.'

'It could be just an ordinary breakdown of some sort,' she said. 'Mechanical failure. They might be making repairs right now.'

'The telephones?'

'Coincidence. Maybe there's nothing sinister about it.'

Suddenly the numerals above the elevator doors in front of them began to light up, one after the other: 16 . . . 17 . . . 18 . . . 19 . . . 20 . . .

'Someone's coming,' Graham said.

A chill passed down her spine.

. . . 25 . . . 26 . . . 27 . . .

'Maybe it's the security guards,' she said.

He said nothing.

She wanted to turn and run, but she could not move. The numbers mesmerized her.

. . . 30 . . . 31 . . . 32 . . .

She thought of women lying in bloody bedclothes, women with their throats cut and their fingers chopped off and their ears cut off.

. . . 33 . . .

'The stairs!' Graham said, startling her.

'Stairs?'

'The emergency stairs.'

. . . 34 . . .

'What about them?'

'We've got to go down.'

'Hide out a few floors below?'

. . . 35 . . .

'No. All the way down to the lobby.'

'That's too far!'

'That's where there's help.'

. . . 36 . . .

'Maybe we don't need help.'

'We need it,' he said.

. . . 37 . . .

'But your leg –'

'I'm not a *complete* cripple,' he said sharply.

. . . 38 . . .

He grabbed her by the shoulder. His fingers hurt her, but she knew he wasn't aware of how fiercely he was gripping her. 'Come on, Connie!'

. . . 39 . . .
Frustrated with her hesitation, he gave her a shove, propelled her out of the alcove. She stumbled, and for an instant she thought she would fall. He kept her upright.

As they hurried down the dark corridor, she heard the elevator doors open behind them.

When Bollinger came out of the elevator alcove, he saw two people running away from him. They were nothing but ghostly shapes, vaguely silhouetted against the eerie glow of the red emergency light at the end of the corridor.

Harris and the woman? he wondered. Have they been alerted? Do they know who I am? How can they know?

'Mr. Harris?' Bollinger called.

They stopped two-thirds of the way down the hall, in front of the open door to the Harris Publications suite. They turned toward him, but he could not see their faces even with the red light spilling over their shoulders.

'Mr. Harris, is that you?'

'Who are you?'

'Police,' Bollinger said. He took a step toward them, then another. As he moved he took the wallet with his badge from his inside coat pocket. With the elevator light behind him, he knew they could see more than he could.

'Don't come any closer,' Harris said.

Bollinger stopped. 'What's the matter?'

'I don't want you to come closer.'

'Why?'

'We don't know who you are.'

'I'm a detective. Frank Bollinger. We have an

appointment for eight-thirty. Remember?' Another step. Then another.

'How did you get up here?' Harris's voice was shrill.

He's scared to death, Bollinger thought. He smiled and said, 'Hey, what's going on with you? Why are you so uptight? You were expecting me.' Bollinger took slow steps, easy steps, so as not to frighten the animals.

'How did you get up here?' Harris asked again. 'The elevators aren't working.'

'You're mistaken. I came up on an elevator.' He held the badge in front of him in his left hand, arm extended, hoping the light from behind would gleam on the gold finish. He had covered perhaps a fifth of the distance between them.

'The telephones are out,' Harris said.

'They are?' Step. Stop.

He put his right hand in his coat pocket and gripped the butt of the pistol.

Connie couldn't take her eyes off the shadowy form moving steadily toward them. To Graham she said softly, 'You remember what you said on the Prine show?'

'What?' His voice cracked.

Don't let the fear take you, she thought. Don't break down and leave me to handle this alone.

She said, 'In your vision you saw that the police know the killer well.'

'What about it?'

'Maybe the Butcher is a cop.'

'Christ, that's it!'

He spoke so softly that she could barely hear him.

Bollinger kept coming, a big man, bearish. His

face was in shadow. He had closed the distance between them by at least half.

'Stop right there,' Graham said. But there was no force in his voice, no authority.

Bollinger stopped anyway. 'Mr. Harris, you're acting very strange. I'm a *policeman*. You know . . . you're acting as if you've just done something that you want to hide from me.' He took a step, another, a third.

'The stairs?' Connie asked.

'No,' Graham said. 'We don't have enough of a lead. With my game leg, he'd catch us in a minute.'

'Mr. Harris?' Bollinger said. 'What are you two saying? Please don't whisper.'

'Where then?' Connie whispered.

'The office.'

He nudged her, and they ducked quickly into the Harris Publications suite, slammed and locked the reception room door.

A second later, Bollinger hit the outside of the door with his shoulder. It trembled in its frame. He rattled the knob violently.

'He's probably got a gun,' Connie said. 'He'll get in sooner or later.'

Graham nodded. 'I know.'

Part three
FRIDAY
8:30–10:30 P.M.

22

Ira Preduski parked at the end of a string of three squad cars and two unmarked police sedans that blocked one half of the two-lane street. Although there was no one in any of the five vehicles, all the engines were running, headlights blazing; the trio of blue-and-whites were crowned with revolving red beacons. Preduski got out of his car and locked it.

A half inch of snow made the street look clean and pretty. As he walked toward the apartment house, Preduski scuffed his shoes against the side-walk, sending up puffs of white flakes in front of him. The wind whipped the falling snow into his back, and cold flakes found their way past his collar. He was reminded of that February, in his fourth year, when his family moved to Albany, New York, where he saw his first winter storm.

A uniformed patrolman in his late twenties was standing at the bottom of the outside steps to the apartment house.

'Tough job you've got tonight,' Preduski said.

'I don't mind it. I like snow.'

'Yeah? So do I.'

'Besides,' the patrolman said, 'it's better standing out here in the cold than up there in all that blood.'

The room smelled of blood, excrement and dusting powder.

Fingers bent like claws, the dead woman lay on the floor beside the bed. Her eyes were open.

Two lab technicians were working around the body, studying it carefully before chalking its position and moving it.

Ralph Martin was the detective handling the on-scene investigation. He was chubby, completely bald, with bushy eyebrows and dark-rimmed glasses. He avoided looking at the corpse.

'The call from the Butcher came in at ten of seven,' Martin said. 'We tried your home number immediately, but we weren't able to get through until almost eight o'clock.'

'My phone was off the hook. I just got out of bed at a quarter past eight. I'm working graveyard.' He sighed and turned away from the corpse. 'What did he say – this Butcher?'

Martin took two folded sheets of paper from his pocket, unfolded them. 'I dictated the conversation, as well as I could recall it, and one of the girls made copies.'

Preduski read the two pages. 'He gave you no clue to who else he's going to kill tonight?'

'Just what's there.'

'This phone call is out of character.'

'And it's out of character for him to strike two nights in a row,' Martin said.

'It's also not like him to kill two women who knew each other and worked together.'

Martin raised his eyebrows. 'You think Sarah Piper knew something?'

'You mean, did she know who killed her friend?'

'Yeah. You think he killed Sarah to keep her from talking?'

'No. He probably just saw both of them at the Rhinestone Palace and couldn't make up his mind which he wanted the most. She didn't know who murdered Edna Mowry. I'd bet my life on that. Of course I'm not the best judge of character you'll ever meet. I'm pretty dense when it comes to people. God knows. Dense as stone. But this time I think I'm right. If she had known, she would have told me. She wasn't the kind of girl who could hide a thing like that. She was open. Forthright. Honest in her way. She was damned nice.'

Glancing at the dead woman's face, which was surprisingly unmarked and clear of blood in the midst of so much gore, Martin said, 'She was lovely.'

'I didn't mean just nice-looking,' Preduski said. 'She was a nice *person*.'

Martin nodded.

'She had a soft Georgia accent that reminded me of home.'

'Home?' Martin was confused. '*You're* from Georgia?'

'Why not?'

'Ira Preduski from Georgia?'

'They *do* have Jews and Slavs down there.'

'Where's your accent?'

'My parents weren't born in the South, so they didn't have an accent to pass on to me. And we moved North when I was four, before I had time to pick it up.'

For a moment they stared at the late Sarah Piper and at the pair of technicians who bent over her like Egyptian attendants of death.

Preduski turned away from the corpse, took a handkerchief from his pocket and blew his nose.

'The coroner's in the kitchen,' Martin said. His face was pale and greasy with sweat. 'He said he wanted to see you when you checked in.'

'Give me a few minutes,' Preduski said. 'I want to look around here a bit and talk with these fellows.'

'Mind if I wait in the living room?'

'No. Go ahead.'

Martin shuddered. 'This is a rotten job.'

'Rotten,' Preduski agreed.

23

The gunshot boomed and echoed in the dark corridor.

The lock shattered, and the wood splintered under the impact of the bullet.

Wrinkling his nose at the odor of burnt powder and scorched metal, Bollinger pushed open the ruined door.

The reception lounge was dark. When he found the light switch and flipped it up, he discovered that the room was also deserted.

Harris Publications occupied the smallest of three business suites on the fortieth floor. In addition to the hall door by which he had entered, two other doors opened from the reception area, one to the left and one to the right. Five rooms. Including the lounge. That didn't leave Harris and the woman with many places to hide.

First he tried the door to the left. It led to a private corridor that served three large offices: one for an editor and his secretary, one for an advertising space salesman, and one for the two-man art department.

Neither Harris nor the woman was in any of those rooms.

Bollinger was cool, calm, but at the same time enormously excited. No sport could be half so dramatic and rewarding as hunting down people. He actually enjoyed the chase more than he did the kill. Indeed, he got an even greater kick out of the first few days immediately *after* a kill than he did from either the hunt or the murder itself. Once the act was done, once blood had been spilled, he had to wonder if he'd made a mistake, if he'd left behind a clue that would lead the police straight to him. The tension kept him sharp, made the juices bubble. Finally, when sufficient time had passed for him to be certain that he had gotten away with murder, a sense of well-being – of great importance, towering superiority, godhood – filled him like a magic elixir flowing into a long-empty pitcher.

The other door connected the reception room and Graham Harris's private office. It was locked.

He stepped back and fired two shots into the lock. The soft metal twisted and tore; chunks of wood spun into the air.

He still could not open it. They had pushed a heavy piece of furniture against the far side.

When he leaned on the door, pushed with all of his strength, he could not budge it; however, he *could* make the unseen piece of furniture rock back and forth on its base. He figured it was something high, at least as wide as the doorway, but not too deep. Perhaps a bookshelf. Something with a high center of gravity. He began to force the door rhythmically: push hard, relax, push hard, relax, push hard . . . The barricade tipped faster and farther each time he wobbled it – and suddenly it fell away from the door with a loud crash and the sound of breaking glass.

Abruptly the air was laden with whiskey fumes.

He squeezed through the door which remained partly blocked. He stepped over the antique bar they had used as a barrier and put his foot in a puddle of expensive Scotch.

The lights were on, but no one was there.

At the far end of the room there was another door. He went to it, opened it. Beyond lay the gloomy fortieth-floor corridor.

While he had wasted time searching the offices, they had slipped back into the hall by this circuitous route, gaining a few minutes lead on him.

Clever.

But not clever enough.

After all, they were nothing but ignorant game, while he was a master hunter.

He laughed softly.

Bathed in red light, Bollinger went to the nearest end of the hall and opened the fire door without making a sound. He stepped onto the landing in the emergency stairwell, closing the door quietly behind him. A dim white bulb burned above the exit on this side.

He heard their footsteps reverberating from below, amplified by the cold concrete walls.

He went to the steel railing and peered into the alternate layers of light and shadow: landings hung with bulbs, and stairs left dark. Ten or twelve flights down, five or six floors below, the woman's hand appeared on the railing, moving along less quickly than it should have. (If he had been in their place, he would have taken the steps two at a time, perhaps even faster.) Because the open core was so narrow – as long as a flight of stairs, but only one yard wide – Bollinger wasn't able to see at an angle into the tiers of steps beneath him. All he could see was the serpentine railing winding to infinity, and nothing of his prey except her white hand. A second later Harris's hand emerged from the velvety shadows, into the light that spilled out from a landing; he gripped the railing, followed the woman through the hazy light and into the darkness once again, descending.

For an instant Bollinger considered going down the steps behind them, shooting them in the back, but he rejected that thought almost as soon as it occurred to him. They would hear him coming. They would most likely scuttle out of the stairwell, seeking a place to hide or another escape route. He wouldn't know for certain at which floor they had left the stairs, and he couldn't run after them and watch their hands on the railing at the same time.

He didn't want to lose track of them. Although he wouldn't mind an interesting and complicated hunt, he didn't want it to drag on all night. For one thing, Billy would be waiting in the car, outside in the alley, at ten o'clock. For another, he wanted time with the woman, at least half an hour if she was at all good-looking.

Her pale hand slipped into sight on a light-swathed patch of railing.

Then Harris's hand.

They were still not moving as fast as they should have.

He tried to count flights of stairs. Twelve to fourteen. . . . They were six, maybe seven floors below.

Where did that put them?

Thirty-third floor?

Bollinger turned away from the railing, opened the door and left the stairwell. He ran down the fortieth-floor corridor to the elevator cab he was using. He switched it on with his key, hesitated, then put his thumb on the button for the twenty-sixth floor.

24

To Connie the stairwell seemed endless. As she passed through alternating levels of purple darkness and wan light, she felt as if she were following a long pathway to hell, the Butcher fulfilling the role of the grinning hellhound that harried her ever downward.

The stale air was cool. Nevertheless, she was perspiring.

She knew they should be going faster, but they were hampered in their flight by Graham's lame left leg. At one point she was almost overcome with anger, furious at him for being a hindrance to their escape. However, her fury vanished in the same instant, leaving her surprised by it and flushed with guilt. She had thought that no pressure, however great, could cause her to react to him so negatively. But filled with – nearly consumed by – the survival instinct, she clearly was capable of responses and attitudes that she would have criticized in others. Extreme circumstances could alter anyone's personality. That insight forced her to understand and appreciate Graham's fear to an extent she had never done before. After all, he had not *wanted* to fall on Everest; he hadn't *asked* for the injury. And indeed, considering the dull pain he suffered when he tried to climb or descend more than two flights of stairs, he was responding to this challenge damned well.

From behind her, Graham said, 'You go on ahead.' He had said it several times before. 'You move faster.'

'I'm staying,' she said breathlessly.

The echoes of their low-pitched voices were eerie, soft and sibilant.

She reached the landing at the thirty-first floor, waited for him to catch up, then went ahead. 'I won't leave you alone. Two of us . . . have a better chance against him . . . better than one of us would.'

'He's got a gun. We've *no* chance.'

She said nothing. She just kept taking the steps one at a time.

'Go on,' he said, sucking breath between phrases. 'You bring back . . . security guard . . . in time to keep . . . him from . . . killing me.'

'I think the guards are dead.'

'What?'

She hadn't wanted to say it, as if saying would make it so. 'How else . . . would he get past them?'

'Sign the registry.'

'And leave his name . . . for the cops to find?'

A dozen steps later he said, 'Christ!'

'What?'

'You're right.'

'No help . . . to be had,' she said. 'We've just got . . . to get out of . . . the building.'

Somehow he found new strength in his left leg. When she reached the thirtieth-floor landing, Connie didn't have to wait for him to catch up.

A minute later, a cannonlike sound boomed up from below, halting them within the fuzzy circle of light at the twenty-ninth floor.

'What was that?'

Graham said, 'A fire door. Someone slammed it . . . down there.'

'Him?'

'*Ssshh.*'

They stood perfectly still, trying to hear movement above the noise of their own labored breathing.

Connie felt as if the circle of light were shrinking around her, rapidly pulling back to a tiny point of brilliance. She was afraid of being blind and helpless, an easy target in pitch blackness. In her mind the Butcher had the quality of a mythical being; he could see in darkness.

As they got control of their breathing, the stairwell became silent.

Too silent.

Unnaturally silent.

Finally Graham said, 'Who's there?'

She jumped, startled by his voice.

The man below said, 'Police, Mr. Harris.'

Under her breath Connie said, 'Bollinger.'

She was at the outer edge of the steps; she looked down the open core. A man's hand was on the railing, four flights below, in the meager illumination just two or three steps up from the landing. She could also see the sleeve of his overcoat.

'Mr. Harris,' Bollinger said. His voice was cold, hollow, distorted by the shaft.

'What do you want?' Graham asked.

'Is she pretty?'

'What?'

'Is she *pretty?*'

'Who?'

'Your woman.'

With that, Bollinger started up. Not hurrying, Leisurely. One step at a time.

She was more frightened by his slow, casual approach than if he had rushed them. By *not* hurrying he was telling them that they were trapped, that he had the whole night to get them if he wished to stretch it out that long.

If only we had a gun, she thought.

Graham took hold of her hand, and they climbed the steps as fast as he was able. It wasn't easy for either of them. Her back and legs ached. With each step, Graham either gritted his teeth or moaned loudly.

When they had gone two floors, four flights, they were forced to stop and rest. He bent over, massaging his bum leg. She went to the railing, peered down.

Bollinger was four flights under them. Evidently he had run when he heard them running; but now he had stopped again. He was leaning over the railing, framed in a pool of light, the gun extended in his right hand.

He smiled at her and said, 'Hey now, you *are* pretty.'

She screamed, jerked back.

He fired.

The shot passed up the core, ricocheted off the top of the rail, smashed into the wall over their heads and ricocheted once more into the steps above them.

She grabbed Graham; he held her.

'I could have killed you,' Bollinger called to her.

'I had you dead on, sweetheart. But you and I are going to have a lot of fun later.'

Then he started up again. As before. Slowly. Shoes scraping ominously on the concrete: *shuss . . . shuss . . . shuss . . . shuss . . .* He began to whistle softly.

'He's not just chasing us,' Graham said angrily. 'The son of a bitch is playing with us.'

'What are we going to do?'

Shuss . . . shuss . . .

'We can't outrun him.'

'But we've got to.'

Shuss . . . shuss . . .

Harris pulled open the landing door. The thirty-first floor lay beyond. 'Come on.'

Not convinced that they gained anything by leaving the stairs, but having nothing better to suggest, she went out of the white light into tho red.

Shuss . . . shuss . . .

Graham shut the door and stooped beside it. A collapsible doorstop was fixed to the bottom right-hand corner of the door. He pushed it all the way down, until the rubber-tipped shank was hard against the floor and the braces were locked in place. His hands were trembling, so that for a moment it looked as if he wouldn't be able to handle even a simple task like this.

'What are you doing?' she asked.

He stood up. 'It might not work if the stop didn't have locking hinges. But it does. See the doorsill? It's an inch higher than the floor on either side. When he tries to open the door, the stop will catch on the sill. It'll be almost as good as a bolt latch.'

'But he's got a gun.'

'Doesn't matter. He can't shoot through a heavy metal fire door.'

Although she was terrified, at the same time Connie was relieved that Graham had taken charge – for however brief a time – and was functioning in spite of his fear.

The door rattled as Bollinger depressed the bar handle on the far side. The stop caught on the sill; its hinges didn't fold up; the door refused to open.

'He'll have to go up or down a floor,' Harris said, 'and come at us by the stairs at the other end of the building. Or by the elevator. Which gives us a few minutes.'

Cursing, Bollinger shook the door, putting all his strength into it. It wouldn't budge.

'What good will a few minutes do us?' Connie asked.

'I don't know.'

'Graham, are we ever going to get out of here?'

'Probably not.'

25

Dr. Andrew Enderby, the medical examiner on the scene, was suave, even dashing, extremely fit for a man in his fifties. He had thick hair going white at the temples. Clear brown eyes. A long aristocratic nose, generally handsome features. His salt-and-pepper mustache was large but well kept. He was wearing a tailored gray suit with tastefully matched accessories that made Preduski's sloppiness all the more apparent.

'Hello, Andy,' Preduski said.

'Number eleven,' Enderby said. 'Unusual. Like numbers five, seven and eight.' When Enderby was excited, which wasn't often, he was impatient to express himself. He sometimes spoke in staccato bursts. He pointed at the kitchen table and said, 'See it? No butter smears. No jelly stains. No crumbs. Too damned neat. Another fake.'

A lab technician was disconnecting the garbage-disposal unit from the pipes under the sink.

'Why?' Preduski said. 'Why does he fake it when he isn't hungry?'

'I know why. Sure of it.'

'So tell me,' Preduski said.

'First of all, did you know I'm a psychiatrist?'

'You're a coroner, a pathologist.'

'Psychiatrist too.'

'I didn't know that.'

'Went to medical school. Did my internship. Specialized in otolaryngology. Couldn't stand it. Hideous way to make a living. My family had money. Didn't have to work. Went back to medical school. Became a psychiatrist.'

'That must be interesting work.'

'Fascinating. But I couldn't stand it. Couldn't stand associating with the patients.'

'Oh?'

'All day with a bunch of neurotics. Began to feel that half of them should be locked up. Got out of the field fast. Better for me *and* the patients.'

'I should say so.'

'Kicked around a bit. Twenty years ago, I became a police pathologist.'

'The dead aren't neurotic.'

'Not even a little bit.'

'And they don't have ear, nose and throat infections.'

'Which they don't pass on to me,' Enderby said. 'No money in this job, of course. But I've got all the money I need. And the work is right for me. I'm perfect for the work, too. My psychiatric training gives me a different perspective. Insights. I have insights that other pathologists might not have. Like the one I had tonight.'

'About why the Butcher sometimes eats a hearty meal and sometimes *fakes* a hearty meal?'

'Yes,' Enderby said. He took a breath. Then: 'It's because there are two of him.'

Preduski scratched his head. 'Schizophrenia?'

'No, no. I mean . . . there isn't just one man running around killing women. There are *two*.' He smiled triumphantly.

Preduski stared at him.

Slamming his fist into his open hand, Enderby said, 'I'm right! I know I am. Butcher number one killed the first four victims. Killing them gave him an appetite. Butcher number two killed the fifth woman. Cut her up as Butcher number one had done. But he was ever so slightly more tender-hearted than the first Butcher. Killing *spoiled* his appetite. So he faked the meal.'

'Why bother to fake it?'

'Simple. He wanted to leave no doubt about who killed her. Wanted us to think it was the Butcher.'

Preduski was suddenly aware of how precisely Enderby's necktie had been knotted. He touched his own tie self-consciously. 'Pardon me. Excuse me. I don't quite understand. My fault. God knows. But, you see, we've never told the newspapers about the scene in the kitchens. We've held that back to check false confessions against real ones. If this guy, Butcher number two, wanted to imitate the real Butcher, how would he know about the kitchen?'

'You're missing my point.'

'I'm sure I am.'

'Butcher number one and Butcher number two know each other. They're in this together.'

Amazed, Preduski said, 'They're friends? You mean they go out and murder – like other men go out bowling?'

'I wouldn't put it like that.'

'They're killing women, trying to make it look like the work of one man?'

'Yes.'

'Why?'

'Don't know. Maybe they're creating a composite character in the Butcher. Giving us an image of a killer that isn't really like either of them. Throw us off the track. Protect themselves.'

Preduski started to pace in front of the littered table. 'Two psychopaths meet in a bar –

'Not necessarily a bar.'

'They get chummy and sign a pact to kill all the women in Manhattan.'

'Not all,' Enderby said. 'But enough.'

'I'm sorry. Maybe I'm not very bright. I'm not well educated. Not a doctor like you. But I can't swallow it. I can't see psychopaths working together so smoothly and effectively.'

'Why not? Remember the Tate murders in California? There were several psychopaths in the Manson family, yet they all worked smoothly and efficiently together, committing a large number of murders.'

'They were caught,' Preduski said.

'Not for quite some time.'

26

Six business offices occupied the thirty-first floor of the Bowerton Building. Graham and Connie tried a few doors, all of which proved to be locked. They knew the others would be shut tight as well.

However, in the main hall near the elevator alcove, Connie discovered an unmarked, unlocked door. She opened it. Graham felt for the light switch, found it. They went inside.

The room was approximately ten feet deep and six or seven feet wide. On the left was a metal door that had been painted bright red; and to one side of the door, mops and brooms and brushes were racked on the wall. On the right, the wall was lined with metal storage shelves full of bathroom and cleaning supplies.

'It's a maintenance center,' Graham said.

Connie went to the red door. She took one step out of the room, holding the door behind her. She was surprised and excited by what she saw. 'Graham! Hey, look at this.'

He didn't respond.

She stepped back into the room, turned and said, 'Graham, look what –'

He was only a foot away, holding a large pair of

scissors up to his face. He gripped the instrument in his fist, in the manner of a man holding a dagger. The blades gleamed; and like polished gems, the sharp points caught the light.

'Graham?' she said.

Lowering the scissors, he said, 'I found these on the shelf over there. I can use them as a weapon.'

'Against a gun?'

'Maybe we can set up a trap.'

'What kind of trap?'

'Lure him into a situation where I can surprise him, where he won't have time enough to use the damned gun.'

'For instance?'

His hand was shaking. Light danced on the blades. 'I don't know,' he said miserably.

'It wouldn't work.' She said. 'Besides, I've found a way out of the building.'

He looked up. 'You have?'

'Come look. You won't need the scissors. Put them down.'

'I'll look,' he said. 'But I'll keep the scissors just in case.'

She was afraid that when he saw the escape route she'd found he would prefer to face the Butcher armed only with the scissors.

He followed her through the red door, onto a railed platform that was only eighteen inches wide and four feet long. A light glowed overhead; and other lights lay some distance away in a peculiar, at first unidentifiable void.

They were suspended on the side of one of the two elevator shafts that went from the ground floor to the roof. It served four cabs, all of which were parked at the bottom. Fat cables dangled in front of Connie and Graham. On this side and on the opposite wall of the cavernous well, from roof to basement at the odd-numbered floors, other doors opened onto other tiny platforms. There was one directly across from Graham and Connie, and the sight of it made them realize the precarious nature of their perch. On both sides of the shaft, metal rungs were bolted to the walls: ladders connecting the doors in each tier to other exits in the same tier.

The system could be used for emergency maintenance work or for moving people off stalled elevators in case of fire, power failure, or other calamity. A small white light burned above each door; otherwise, the shaft would have been in absolute darkness. When Connie looked up, and especially when she looked down from the thirty-first floor, the sets of farther lights appeared to be closer together than the sets of nearer lights. It was a long way to the bottom.

His voice wavered when he said, '*This* is a way out?'

She hesitated then said, 'We can climb down.'

'No.'

'We can't use the stairs. He'll be watching those.'

'Not this.'

'It won't be like mountain climbing.'

His eyes shifted quickly from left to right and back again. 'No.'

'We'll have the ladder.'

'And we'll climb down thirty-one floors?' he asked.

'Please. Graham. If we start now, we might make it. Even if he finds that the maintenance room is unlocked, and even if he sees this red door – well, he might not think we'd have enough nerve to climb down the shaft. And if he *did* see us, we could get off the ladder, leave the shaft at another floor. We'd gain more time.'

'I can't.' He was gripping the railing with both hands, and with such force that she would not have been surprised if the metal had bent like paper in his hands.

Exasperated, she said, 'Graham, what *else* can we do?'

He stared into the concrete depths.

When Bollinger found that Harris and the woman had locked the fire door, he ran down two flights to the thirtieth floor. He intended to use that corridor to reach the far end of the building where he could take the second stairwell back up to the thirty-first level and try the *other* fire door. However, at the next landing the words 'Hollowfield Land Management' were stenciled in black letters on the gray door: the entire floor belonged to a single occupant. That level had no public corridor; the fire door could be opened only from the inside. The same was true of the twenty-ninth and twenty-eight floors, which were the domain of Sweet Sixteen Cosmetics. He tried both entrances without success.

Worried that he would lose track of his prey, he rushed back to the twenty-sixth floor. That was where he had originally entered the stairwell, where he had left the elevator cab.

As he pulled open the fire door and stepped into the hall, he looked at his watch. 9:15. The time was passing too fast, unnaturally fast, as if the universe had become unbalanced.

Hurrying to the elevator alcove, he fished in his pocket for the dead guard's keys. They snagged on the lining. When he jerked them loose, they spun out of his hand and fell on the carpet with a sleighbell jingle.

He knelt and felt for them in the darkness. Then he remembered the pencil flashlight, but even with that he needed more than a minute to locate the keys.

As he got up, angry with himself, he wondered if Harris and the woman were waiting here for him. He put away the flashlight and snatched the pistol from his pocket. He stood quite still. He studied the darkness. If they were hiding there, they would have been silhouetted by the bright spot farther along at the alcove.

When he thought about it, he realized that they couldn't have known on which floor he'd left the elevator. Furthermore, they couldn't have gotten down here in time to surprise him.

The thirty-first floor was a different story. They might have time to set a trap for him up there. When the elevator doors slid open, they might be waiting for him; he would be most vulnerable at that moment.

Then again, *he* was the one with the pistol. So what if they were waiting with makeshift weapons? They didn't stand a chance of overpowering him.

At the elevator he put the key in the control board and activated the circuit.

He looked at his watch. 9:19.

If there were no more delays, he could kill Harris and still have twenty minutes or half an hour with the woman.

Whistling again, he pushed one of the buttons: 31.

The lab technician disconnected the [illegible] for disposal, wrapped it [illegible] [illegible] and carried it out of the [illegible].

Preduski and [illegible] [illegible] [illegible] [illegible] [illegible] kitchen.

In the [illegible] [illegible] [illegible] [illegible] quarter hour: two [illegible] [illegible] [illegible] late. In accompaniment [illegible] [illegible] through the eaves [illegible]

'If you find [illegible] [illegible] chopthe [illegible] [illegible] said, 'then [illegible] [illegible] psychopaths [illegible] [illegible]

'Now you [illegible]

'I know.'

'The Butcher [illegible] [illegible] [illegible] wouldn't know [illegible] [illegible] [illegible] the symptoms of his [illegible] [illegible] how to conceal them. [illegible] [illegible] exam. Harris [illegible]

'I'm beginning [illegible] [illegible]

Except you say there are two Butchers.

Enderby nodded.

Predaski sighed [illegible] [illegible]

27

The lab technician disconnected the garbage disposal, wrapped it in a heavy white plastic sheet, and carried it out of the apartment.

Preduski and Enderby were left alone in the kitchen.

In the foyer, a grandfather clock struck the quarter hour: two soft chimes, running five minutes late. In accompaniment, the wind fluted musically through the eaves just above the kitchen windows.

'If you find it hard to accept the idea of two psychopaths working so smoothly together,' Enderby said, 'then consider the possibility that they aren't psychopaths of any sort we've seen before.'

'Now you sound like Graham Harris.'

'I know.'

'The Butcher is mentally ill, Harris says. But you wouldn't know it to look at him, Harris says. Either the symptoms of his mania don't show, or he knows how to conceal them. He'd pass any psychiatric exam, Harris says.'

'I'm beginning to agree with him.'

Except you say there are two Butchers.'

Enderby nodded.

Preduski sighed. He went to the nearest window

and drew the outline of a knife in the thin gray-white film of moisture that coated the glass. 'If you're right, I can't hold onto my theory. That he's just your ordinary paranoid schizophrenic. Maybe a lone killer could be operating in a psychotic fugue. But not two of them simultaneously.'

'They're not suffering any psychotic fugue,' Enderby agreed. 'Both of these men know precisely what they're doing. Neither of them suffers from amnesia.'

Turning from the window, from the drawing of the knife which had begun to streak as droplets of water slid down the pane, Preduski said, 'Whether this is a new type of psychotic or not, the crime is familiar. Sex murders are –'

'These aren't sex murders,' Enderby said.

Preduski cocked his head. 'Come again?'

'These aren't *sex* murders.'

'They only kill women.'

'Yes, but –'

'And they rape them first.'

'Yes. It's murder with sex *associated*. But these aren't *sex* murders.'

'I'm sorry. I'm lost. My fault. Not yours.'

'Sex isn't the motivating force. Sex isn't the whole or even the primary reason they have for attacking these women. The opportunity for rape is there. So they take it. Going to kill the women anyway. They aren't adding to their legal risks by raping them first. Sex is secondary. They aren't killing out of some psychosexual impulse.'

Shaking his head, Preduski said, 'I don't see how you can say that. You've never met them. What evidence do you have that their motives aren't basically sexual?'

'Circumstantial,' Enderby said. 'For instance, the way they mutilate the corpses.'

'What about it?'

'Have you studied the mutilations carefully?'

'I had no choice.'

'All right. Found any sign of anal mutilation?'

'No.'

'Mutilation of the genitalia?'

'No.'

'Mutilation of the breasts?'

'In some cases he's cut open the abdomen and chest cavity.'

'Mutilation of the breasts alone?'

'When he opens the chest –'

'I mean has he ever cut off a woman's nipples, or perhaps her entire breasts, as Jack the Ripper did?'

A look of loathing came over his face. 'No.'

'Has he ever mutilated the mouth of a victim?'

'The mouth?'

'Has he ever cut off the lips?'

'No. Never.'

'Has he ever cut out a tongue?'

'God, no! Andy, do we have to go on like this? It's morbid. And I don't see where it's leading.'

'If they were maniacal sex killers with a desire to cut their victims,' Enderby said, 'they'd have disfigured one of those areas.'

'Anus, breasts, genitalia or mouth?'

'Unquestionably. At least one of them. Probably all of them. But they didn't. So the mutilation is an after thought. Not a sexual compulsion. Window dressing.'

Preduski closed his eyes, pressed his fingertips to them, as if he were trying to suppress unpleasant images. 'Window dressing? I'm afraid I don't understand.'

'To impress us.'

'The police?'

'Yes. And the newspapers.'

Preduski went to the window where he had drawn the knife. He wiped away the film of moisture and stared at the snow sheeting through the glow around the street lamp. 'Why would he want to impress us?'

'I don't know. Whatever the reason, whatever the need behind his desire to impress – *that* is the true motivation.'

'If we knew what it was, we might be able to see a pattern in the killings. We might be able to anticipate him.'

Suddenly excited, Enderby said, 'Wait a minute. Another case. Two killers. Working together. Chicago. Nineteen twenty-four. Two young men were the murderers. Both sons of millionaires. In their late teens.'

'Leopold and Loeb.'

'You know the case?'

'Slightly.'

'They killed a boy, Bobby Franks. Fourteen years old. Son of another rich man. They had nothing against him. None of the usual reasons. No classic motive. Newspapers said it was for kicks. For thrills. Very bloody murder. But they killed Franks for other reasons. For more than kicks. For a philosophical ideal.'

Turning away from the window, Preduski said, 'I'm sorry. I must have missed something. I'm not making sense of this. *What* philosophical ideal?'

'They thought they were special. Supermen. The

first of a new race. Leopold idolized Nietzsche.'

Frowning, Preduski said, 'One of the quotes in there on the bedroom wall is probably from Nietzsche's work, the other from Blake. There was a quote from Nietzsche written in blood on Edna Mowry's wall last night.'

'Leopold and Loeb. Incredible pair. They thought that committing the perfect crime was proof that they were supermen. Getting away with murder. They thought that was *proof* of superior intelligence, superior cunning.'

'Weren't they homosexuals?'

'Yes. But that doesn't make Bobby Franks the victim of a sex killing. They didn't molest him. Never had any intention of molesting him. They weren't motivated by lust. Not at all. It was, as Loeb called it, "an intellectual exercise." '

In spite of his excitement, Enderby noticed that his shirt cuffs were not showing beyond the sleeves of his suit jacket. He pulled them out, one at a time, until the proper half inch was revealed. Although he had worked for some time in the blood-splashed bedroom and then in the messy kitchen, he didn't have a stain on him.

His back to the window, leaning against the sill, conscious of his own scuffed shoes and wrinkled trousers, Preduski said, 'I'm having trouble understanding. You'll have to be patient with me. You know how I am. Dense sometimes. But if these two boys, Leopold and Loeb, thought that murder was an intellectual exercise, then they were crazy. Weren't they? Were they mad?'

'In a way. Mad with their own power. Both real and imagined power.'

'Would they have appeared to be mad?'

'Not at all.'

'How is that possible?'

'Remember, Leopold graduated from college when he was just seventeen. He had an IQ of two hundred or nearly so. He was a genius. So was Loeb. They were bright enough to keep their Nietzschean fantasies to themselves, to hide their grandiose self-images.'

'What if they'd taken psychiatric tests?'

'Psychiatric tests weren't very well developed in nineteen twenty-four.'

'But if there had been tests back then as sophisticated as those we have today, would Leopold and Loeb have passed them?'

'Probably with flying colors.'

'Have there been others like Leopold and Loeb since nineteen twenty-four?' Preduski asked.

'Not that I know of. Not in a pure sense, anyway. The Manson family killed for murky political and religious reasons. They thought Manson was Christ. Thought killing the rich would help the downtrodden. Unmitigated crazies, in my book. Think of some other killers, especially mass murderers. Charles Starkweather. Richard Speck. Albert DeSalvo. All of them were psychotic. All of them were driven by psychoses that had grown and festered in them, that had slowly corrupted them since childhood. In Leopold and Loeb, there were apparently no serious childhood traumas that could have led to psychotic behavior. No black seed to bear fruit later.'

'So if the Butcher is two men,' Preduski said forlornly, 'we've got a new Leopold and Loeb. Killing to prove their superiority.'

Enderby began to pace. 'Maybe. But then again,

maybe it's more than that. Something more complex than that.'

'Like what?'

'I don't know. But I feel it's not *exactly* a Leopold and Loeb sort of thing.' He went to the table and stared at the remains of the meal that had never been eaten. 'Have you called Harris?'

Preduski said, 'No.'

'You should. He's been trying to get an image of the killer. Hasn't had any luck. Maybe that's because he's focusing on a single image, trying to envision just one face. Tell him there are *two* killers. Maybe that'll break it open for him. Maybe he'll finally get a handle on the case.'

'We don't *know* there are two. That's just a theory.'

'Tell him anyway,' Enderby said. 'What harm can it do?'

'I should tell him tonight. I really should. But I just can't,' Preduski said. 'He's gotten behind in his work because of this case. That's my fault. I'm always calling him, talking to him, pressuring him about it. He's working late, trying to get caught up. I don't want to disturb him.'

In the foyer by the front door, the grandfather clock chimed the half hour, five minutes late again.

Preduski glanced at his wristwatch and said, 'It'll soon be ten o'clock. I've got to be going.'

'Going? There's work to do here.'

'I'm not on duty yet.'

'Graveyard?'

'Yeah.'

'I never knew you to hesitate about a bit of overtime.'

'Well, I just got out of bed. I was cooking spaghetti when Headquarters called me about this. Never got a chance to eat any of it. I'm starving.'

Enderby shook his head. 'As long as I've known you, I don't believe I've ever seen you eat a square meal. You're always grabbing sandwiches so you don't have to stop working to eat. And at home you're cooking spaghetti. You need a wife, Ira.'

'A wife?'

'Other men have them.'

'But me? Are you kidding?'

'Be good for you.'

'Andy, look at me.'

'I'm looking.'

'Look closer.'

'So?'

'You must be blind.'

'What should I see?'

'What woman in her right mind would marry me?'

'Don't give me your usual crap, Ira,' Enderby said with a smile. 'I know that under all of that self-deprecating chatter, you've got a healthy and proper respect for yourself.'

'You're the psychiatrist.'

'That's right. I'm not a suspect or a witness; you can't charm me with that blather.'

Preduski grinned.

'I'll bet there have been more than a few women who've fallen for that calculated little-boy look of yours.'

'A few,' Preduski admitted uncomfortably. 'But never the *right* woman.'

'Who said anything about the *right* one? Most men are happy to settle for half-right.'

'Not me.' Preduski looked at his watch again. 'I

really have to be going. I'll come back around midnight. Martin probably won't even have finished questioning the other tenants by then. It's a big building.'

Dr Enderby sighed as if the troubles of the world were on his shoulders alone. 'We'll be here too. Dusting the furniture for prints, vacuuming the carpets for hairs and threads, finding nothing, but working hard. The same old circus.'

28

Graham's foot slipped off the rung.

Although he was still holding tightly with both hands, he panicked. He struck out at the ladder with his feet, scrabbling wildly, as if the ladder were alive, as if he had to kick it into submission before he could regain his foothold on it.

'Graham, what's wrong?' Connie asked from her position on the ladder above him. 'Graham?'

Her voice sobered him. He stopped kicking. He hung by his hands until he was breathing almost normally, until the vivid memories of Everest had faded.

'Graham?'

With his feet he probed for a rung, found one after several seconds that seemed like hours. 'I'm all right. My foot slipped. I'm okay now.'

'Don't look down.'

'I didn't. I won't.'

He sought the next rung, stepped to it, continued the descent.

He felt feverish. The hair was damp at the back of his neck. Perspiration beaded his forehead, jeweled his eyebrows, stung the corners of his eyes, filmed his cheeks, brought a salty taste to his lips.

In spite of the perspiration, he was cold. He shivered as he moved down the long ladder.

He was as much aware of the void at his back as he would have been of a knife pressed between his shoulder blades.

On the thirty-first floor, Frank Bollinger entered the maintenance supply room.

He saw the red door. Someone had put down the doorstop that was fixed to it, so that it was open an inch or two. He knew immediately that Harris and the woman had gone through there.

But why was the door ajar?

It was like a signpost. Beckoning him.

Alert for a trap, he advanced cautiously. He held the Walther PPK in his right hand. He kept his left hand out in front of him, arm extended all the way, to stop the door in case they tried to throw it open in his face. He held his breath for those few steps, listening for the slightest sound other than the soft squeak of his own shoes.

Nothing. Silence.

He used the toe of his shoe to push up the doorstop; then he pulled open the door and walked onto the small platform. He had just enough time to realize where he was, when the door closed behind him and all the lights in the shaft went out.

At first he thought Harris had come into the maintenance room after him. But when he tried the door, it was not locked. And when he opened it, all the lights came on. The emergency lighting didn't burn twenty-four hours a day; it came on only when one of the service entrances was open; and that was why Harris had left the door ajar.

Bollinger was impressed by the system of lights

and platforms and ladders. Not every building erected in the 1920s would have been designed with an eye toward emergencies. In fact, damned few skyscrapers built since the war could boast *any* safety provisions. These days, they expected you to wait in a stalled elevator until it was repaired, no matter if that took ten hours or ten days; and if the lift couldn't be repaired, you could risk a manually cranked descent, or you could rot in it.

The more time he spent in the building, the deeper he penetrated it, the more fascinating he found it to be. It was not on the scale of those truly gargantuan stadiums and museums and highrises that Hitler had designed for the 'super race' just prior to and during the first days of World War Two. But then Hitler's magnificent edifices had never been realized in stone and mortar, whereas this place *had* risen. He began to feel that the men who had designed and constructed it were Olympians. He found his appreciation strange, for he knew that had he been restricted to the halls and offices during the day, when the building was full of people and buzzing with commerce, he would not have noticed the great size and high style of the structure. One took for granted that which was commonplace; and to New Yorkers, there was nothing unusual about a forty-two-story office building. Now, however, abandoned for the night, the tower seemed incredibly huge and complex; in solitude and silence one had time to contemplate it and to see how magnificent and extraordinary it was. He was like a microbe wandering through the veins and bowels of a living creature, a behemoth almost beyond measurement.

He felt in league with the minds that could conceive of a monument like this. He was one of them, a mover and shaker, a superior man. The Olympian nature of the building – and of the architects responsible for it – struck a responsive chord in him, made him reverberate with the knowledge of his own special godlike stature. Brimming with a sense of glory, he was more determined than ever to kill Harris and the woman. They were animals. Lice. Parasites. Because of Harris's freakish psychic gift, they posed a threat to Bollinger. They were trying to deny him his rightful place in this new and forceful current of history: the at first gradual but ever-quickening rise of the new men.

He pushed the doorstop against the floor to keep the door open and the lights burning. Then he went to the edge of the platform and peered down the ladder.

They were three floors under him. The woman on top, nearest by a few rungs. Harris below her, going first. Neither of them looked up. They certainly were aware of the momentary loss of light and understood the significance of it. They were hurrying toward the next platform, where they could get out of the shaft.

Bollinger knelt, tested the railing. It was strong. He leaned against it, using it like a safety harness to keep him from tumbling to his death.

He didn't want to kill them here. The place and method of murder were extremely important tonight. Here, they would drop to the bottom of the well, and that would ruin the scheme that he and Billy had come up with this afternoon. He wasn't here just to kill them any way he could; he had to dispose of them in a certain manner. If he brought it off just right, the police would be confused, misled; and the people of New York would begin to experience a spiraling reign of terror unlike anything in their worst nightmares. He and Billy had worked out a damned clever gambit, and he wouldn't abandon it so long as there was a chance of bringing it off as planned.

It was a quarter of ten. In fifteen minutes Billy would be in the alleyway outside, and he would wait only until ten-thirty. Bollinger saw that he probably wouldn't have time for the woman, but he was pretty sure he'd be able to carry out the plan in forty-five minutes.

Besides, he didn't know what Harris looked like, and he felt there was something cowardly about killing a man whose face he'd never seen. It was akin to shooting someone in the back. That sort of killing - even of an animal, even of a louse like Harris - didn't fit Bollinger's image of a superman. He liked to meet his prey head-on, to get close, so that there was at least a hint of danger.

The trick was to force them out of the shaft without killing them; to herd them to other ground where the plan could be carried out. He pointed the pistol down, aimed wide of the woman's head and squeezed the trigger.

The shot exploded; ear-splitting noise assaulted Connie from every side. Over the diminishing echoes, she could hear the bullet ricocheting from one wall to the other, farther down the shaft.

The situation was so unreal that she had to wonder if it was transpiring in her mind. She supposed it was possible that she was in a hospital and that all of this was the product of a fevered imagination, the delusions of madness.

Descending the ladder, she repeatedly caught herself murmuring softly: sometimes it was jumbled phrases that made little sense, sometimes strings of utterly meaningless sounds. Her stomach rolled over like a fish on a wet boat dock. Her bowels quivered. She felt as if a bullet had already ripped into her, already had torn apart her vital organs.

Bollinger fired again.

The shot seemed less sharp than the one before it. Her ears were desensitized, still ringing from the first explosion.

For a woman who had experienced little emotional - and *no* physical - terror in her life, she was handling herself surprisingly well.

When she looked down, she saw Graham let go of the ladder with one hand. He grabbed the railing that ringed the platform. He took one foot off the ladder; hesitated, leaning at a precarious angle; started to bring his foot back; suddenly found the courage to put it on the edge of the platform. For a moment, fighting his own terror, he stayed that way, crucified between the two points of safety. She was about to call to him, urge him on, when he finally freed himself of the ladder altogether, wobbled on the brink of the platform as if he would fall, then got his balance and climbed over the railing.

She descended the last dozen rungs much too fast and reached the platform as Bollinger fired a third shot. She hurried through the red door that Graham held open for her, into the maintenance supply room on the twenty-seventh level.

The first thing she saw was the blood on his trousers. A bright spot of it. As big as a silver dollar. Glistening on the gray fabric. 'What happened?'

'Had these in my pocket,' he said, holding up the scissors. 'A couple of floors back, when I almost fell, the blades tore through the lining and gouged my thigh.'

'Is it bad?'

'No.'

'Hurt?'

'Not much.'

'Better get rid of them.'

'Not just yet.'

Bollinger watched until they left the shaft. They had gotten out two platforms down. Because there was only a service entrance at every second floor, that put them on the twenty-seventh level.

He got up, hurried toward the elevator.

'Come on,' Graham said. 'Let's make a run for the stairs.'

'No. We've got to go back up the shaft.'

Incredulity showed on his face, anguish in his eyes. 'That's crazy!'

'He won't be looking for us in the shaft. At least not for a couple of minutes. We can go up two floors, then use the stairs when he comes back to check the shaft.' She opened the red door through which they'd come only seconds ago.

'I don't know if I can do it again,' he said.

'Of course you can.'

'You said *up* the shaft?'

'That's right.'

'We have to go down to escape.'

She shook her head; her hair formed a brief dark halo. 'You remember what I said about the night guards?'

'They might be dead.'

'If Bollinger killed them so he could have a free hand with us, wouldn't he also have sealed off the building? What if we get to the lobby, with Bollinger hot on our heels, and we find the doors are locked? Before we could break the glass and get out, he'd have killed us.'

'But the guards might not be dead. He might have gotten past them somehow.'

'Can we take that chance?'

He frowned. 'I guess not.'

'I don't want to get to the lobby until we're certain of having a long lead on Bollinger.'

'So we go up. How's that better?'

'We can't play cat and mouse with him for twenty-seven floors. The next time he catches us in the shaft or on the stairs, he won't make any mistakes. But if he doesn't realize we're going *up*, we might be able to alternate between the shaft and the stairs for thirteen floors, long enough to get to your office.'

'Why there?'

'Because he won't expect us to backtrack.'

Graham's blue eyes were not as wide with fear as they had been; they had narrowed with calculation. In spite of himself, the will to survive was flowering in him; the first signs of the old Graham Harris were becoming visible, pushing through his shell of fear.

He said, 'Eventually, he'll realize what we've done. It'll buy us only fifteen minutes or so.'

'Time to think of another way out,' she said. 'Come on, Graham. We're wasting too much time. He'll be on this floor any second now.'

Less reluctantly than the first time, but still

without enthusiasm, he followed her into the elevator shaft.

On the platform he said, 'You go first. I'll bring up the rear, so I won't knock you off the ladder if I fall.'

For the same reason, he had insisted on going first when they descended.

She put her arms around him, kissed him, then turned and started to climb.

As soon as he got off the elevator on the twenty-seventh floor, Bollinger investigated the stairs at the north end of the building. They were deserted.

He ran the length of the corridor and opened the door to the south stairs. He stood on the landing for almost a minute, listening intently for movement. He heard none.

In the corridor again, he searched for an unlocked office door until he realized they might have gone back into the elevator shaft. He located the maintenance supply room; the red door was ajar.

He approached it cautiously, as before. He was opening the door all the way when the shaft beyond was filled with the sound of another door closing on it.

On the platform, he bent over the railing. He stared down into the vertiginous depths, wondering which one of the doors they had used.

How many floors had they gained on him?

Dammit!

Cursing aloud, overcoat flapping around his legs, Bollinger went back to the south stairs to listen for them.

* * *

By the time they had climbed two flights on the north stairs, Graham was wincing with each step. From sole to hip, pain coruscated through his bad leg. In anticipation of each jolt, he tensed his stomach. Now his entire abdomen ached. If he had continued to work out and climb after his fall on Mount Everest, as the doctors had urged him to do, he would have been in shape for this. He had given his leg more punishment tonight than it ordinarily received in a year. Now he was paying in pain for five years of inactivity.

'Don't slow down,' Connie said.

'Trying not to.'

'Use the rail as much as you can. Pull yourself along.'

'How far are we going?'

'One more floor.'

'Eternity.'

'After that we'll switch back to the elevator shaft.'

He liked the ladder in the shaft better than he did the stairs. On the ladder he could use his good leg and pull with both hands to keep nearly all of his weight off the other leg. But on the stairs, if he didn't use the lame leg at all, he would have to hop from one step to the other; and that was too slow.

'One more flight,' she said encouragingly.

Trying to surprise himself, trying to cover a lot of ground before the pain transmitted itself from leg to brain, he put on a burst of speed, staggered up ten steps as fast as he could. That transformed the pain into agony. He had to slow down, but he kept moving.

Bollinger stood on the landing, listening for sound in the south stairwell.

Nothing.

He looked over the railing. Squinting, he tried to see through the layers of darkness that filled the space between the landings.

Nothing.

He went back into the hall and ran toward the north stairs.

29

Billy drove into the alley. His car made the first tracks in the new snow.

A forty-foot-long, twenty-foot-deep service courtyard lay at the back of the Bowerton Building. Four doors opened onto it. One of these was a big green garage door, where delivery could be taken on office furniture and other items too large to fit through the public entrance. A sodium vapor lamp glowed above the green door, casting a harsh light on the stone walls, on the rows of trash bins awaiting pickup in the morning, and on the snow; the shadows were sharply drawn.

There was no sign of Bollinger.

Prepared to leave at the first indication of trouble, Billy backed the car into the courtyard. He switched off the headlights but not the engine. He rolled down his window, just an inch, to keep the glass from steaming up.

When Bollinger didn't come out to meet him, Billy looked at his watch. 10:02.

Clouds of dry snow swirled down the alley in front of him. In the courtyard, out of the worst of the wind, the snow was relatively undisturbed.

Most nights, squad cars conducted random

patrols of poorly lighted back streets like this one, always on the lookout for business-district burglars with half-filled vans, muggers with half-robbed victims, and rapists with half-subdued women. But not tonight. Not in this weather. The city's uniformed patrolmen would be occupied elsewhere. The majority of them would be busy cleaning up after the usual foul-weather automobile accidents, but as much as a third of the evening shift would be squirreled away in favorite hideouts, on a side street or in a park; they would be drinking coffee – in a few cases, something stronger – and talking about sports and women, ready to go to work only if the radio dispatcher insisted upon it.

Billy looked at his watch again. 10:04.

He would wait exactly twenty-six minutes. Not one minute less, and certainly not one more. That was what he had promised Dwight.

Once again, Bollinger reached the elevator shaft just as it was filled with the sound of another door closing on it.

He bent over the railing, looked down. Nothing but other railings, other platforms, other emergency light bulbs, and a lot of darkness. Harris and the woman had gone.

He was tired of playing hide-and-seek with them, of dashing from stairwell to stairwell to shaft. He was sweating profusely. Under his overcoat, his shirt clung to him wetly. He left the platform, went to the elevator, activated it with a key, pushed the button marked 'Lobby.'

On the ground level, he took off his heavy overcoat and dropped it beside the elevator doors. Sweat trickled down his neck, down the center of his chest. He didn't remove his gloves. With the back of his left hand and then with his shirt sleeve he wiped his dripping forehead.

Out of sight of anyone who might come to the street doors, he leaned against the marble wall at the end of the offset that contained the four banks of elevators. From that position, he could see two white doors with black stenciled letters on them, one at the north end and one at the south end of the lobby. These were the exits from the stairwells. When Harris and the woman came through one of them, he would blow their goddamned brains out. Oh, yes. With pleasure.

Hobbling along the fortieth-floor corridor toward the light that came from the open reception-room door of the Harris Publications suite, Harris saw the fire-alarm box. It was approximately nine inches on a side, set flush with the wall. The metal rim was painted red, and the face of it was glass.

He couldn't imagine why he hadn't thought of this before.

Ahead of him, Connie realized that he had stopped. 'What's the matter?'

'Look here.'

She came back.

'If we set it off,' Graham said, 'it'll bring the security guards up from downstairs.'

'If they aren't dead.'

'Even if they are dead, it'll bring the fire department on the double. Bollinger will have the crimps put to him.'

'Maybe he won't run when he hears the bells. After all, we know his name. He might hang on, kill us, sneak out past the firemen.'

'He might,' Graham agreed, unsettled by the thought of being stalked through dark halls full of clanging, banging bells.

They stared through the glass at the steel alarm lever that glinted in the red light.

He felt hope, like a muscle relaxant, relieve a fraction of the tension in his shoulders, neck and face. For the first time all night, he began to think they might escape.

Then he remembered the vision. The bullet. The blood. He was going to be shot in the back.

She said, 'The alarms will probably be so loud that we won't hear him if he comes after us.'

'But it works both ways,' he said eagerly. '*He* won't be able to hear us.'

She pressed her fingertips to the cool plate of glass, hesitated, then took her hand away. 'Okay. But there's no little hammer to break the glass.' She held up the chain that was supposed to secure a hammer to the side of the alarm. 'What do we use instead?'

Smiling, he took the scissors from his pocket and held them up as if they were a talisman.

'Applause, applause,' she said, beginning to feel just enough hope to allow herself a little joke.

'Thank you.'

'Be careful,' she said.

'Stand back.'

She did.

Graham held the scissors by the closed blades. Using the heavy handles as a hammer, he smashed the thin glass. A few pieces held stubbornly to the frame. So as not to cut himself, he broke out the jagged splinters before he put one hand into the shallow alarm box and jerked the steel lever from green to red.

No noise.

No bells.

Silence.

Christ!

'Oh, no,' she said.

Frantically, the flame of hope flickering in him, he pushed the lever up, back to the green safety mark, then slammed it down again.

Still nothing.

Bollinger had been as thorough with the fire alarm as he had been with the telephones.

The wipers swept back and forth, clearing the snow from the windshield. The rhythmic *thump-thump-thump* was getting on his nerves.

Billy glanced over his shoulder, through the rear window, at the green garage door, then at the other three doors.

The time was 10:15.

Where in the hell was Dwight?

Graham and Connie went to the magazine's art department in search of a knife and other sharp draftsmen's tools that would make better weapons than the scissors. He found a pair of razor-edged scalpel-like instruments in the center drawer of the art director's big metal desk.

When he looked up from the drawer, he saw that Connie was lost in thought. She was standing just inside the door, staring at the floor in front of a light blue photographic backdrop. Climbing equipment - coils of rope, pitons, étriers, carabiners, klettershoes, nylon jackets lined with down, and perhaps thirty other items – lay in a disordered heap before the screen.

'See what I found?' he said. He held up the blades.

She wasn't interested. 'What about this stuff?' she asked, pointing to the climbing equipment.

Coming from behind the desk, he said, 'This issue, we're running a buyer's guide. Each of those pieces was photographed for the article. Why'd you ask?' Then his face brightened. 'Never mind. I see why.' He hunkered in front of the equipment, picked up an ice ax. 'This makes a better weapon than any draftsman's tool.'

'Graham?'

He looked up.

Her expression was peculiar: a combination of puzzlement, fear and amazement. Although she clearly had thought of something interesting and important, her gray eyes gave no indication of what was going through her mind. She said, 'Let's not rush out to fight him. Can we consider all of our options?'

'That's why we're here.'

She stepped into the short, private hallway, cocked her head and listened for Bollinger.

Graham stood up, prepared to use the ice ax.

When she was satisfied that there was nothing to listen for but more silence, she came back into the room.

He lowered the ax. 'I thought you heard something.'

'Just being cautious.' She glanced at the climbing equipment before she sat down on the edge of the desk. 'As I see it, there are five different things we can do. Number one, we can make a stand, try to fight Bollinger.'

'With this,' he said, hefting the ice ax.

'And with anything else we can find.'

'We can set a trap, surprise him.'

'I see two problems with that approach.'

'The gun.'

'That's sure one.'

'If we're clever enough, he won't have time to shoot.'

'More important,' she said, 'neither of us is a killer.'

'We could just knock him unconscious.'

'If you hit him on the head with an ax like that, you're bound to kill him.'

'If it's kill or be killed, I suppose I could do it.'

'Maybe. But if you hesitate at the last instant, we're dead.'

He didn't resent the limits of her faith in him; he knew that he didn't deserve her complete trust. 'You said there were five things we could do.'

'Number two, we can try to hide.'

'Where?'

'I don't know. Maybe look for an office that someone forgot to lock, go inside and lock it after us.'

'No one forgot.'

'Maybe we *can* continue to play cat and mouse with him.'

'For how long?'

'Until a new shift of guards finds the dead ones.'

'If he didn't kill the guards, then the new guards won't know what's going on up here.'

'That's right.'

'Besides, I think maybe they work twelve-hour shifts, four days a week. I know one of the night men. I've heard him curse the long shifts and at the same time praise the eight hours of overtime he gets each week. So if they come on duty at six, they won't be off until six in the morning.'

'Seven and a half hours.'

'Too long to play cat and mouse in the elevator shaft and on the stairs. Especially with this bum leg of mine.'

'Number three,' she said. 'We could open one of your office windows and shout for help.'

'From the fortieth floor? Even in good weather, they probably couldn't hear you on the sidewalk. With this wind, they wouldn't hear you even two floors away.'

'I know that. And on a night like this, there's not going to be anyone out walking anyway.'

'Then why'd you suggest it?'

'Number five is going to surprise you,' she said. 'When I get to it, I want you to understand that I've thought of every other possible out.'

'What's number five?'

'Number four first. We open the office window and throw furniture into the street, try to catch the attention of anyone who's driving past on Lexington.'

'If anyone *is* driving in this weather.'

'Someone will be. A taxi or two.'

'But if we toss out a chair, we won't be able to calculate the effect of the wind on it. We won't be able to gauge where it'll land. What if it goes through the windshield of a car and kills someone?'

'I've thought of that.'

'We can't do it.'

'I know.'

'What's number five?'

She slid off the desk and went to the pile of climbing equipment. 'We've got to get rigged out in this stuff.'

'Rigged out?'

'Boots, jackets, gloves, ropes – the works.'

He was perplexed. 'Why?'

Her eyes were wide, like the eyes of a startled doe. 'For the climb down.'

'Down what?'

'Down the outside of the building. All the way to the street.'

Part four

FRIDAY 10:30 P.M.–
SATURDAY 4:00 A.M.

30

Promptly at ten-thirty, Billy drove out of the service courtyard behind the highrise.

The snowfall had grown heavier during the past half hour, and the wind had become downright dangerous. Roiling in the headlight beams, the sheets of powder-dry flakes were almost as dense as a fog.

At the mouth of the alley, as he was pulling onto the side street, the tires spun on the icy pavement. The car slewed toward the far curb. He turned the wheel in the direction of the slide and managed to stop just short of colliding with a panel truck parked at the curb.

He had been driving too fast, and he hadn't even been aware of it until he'd almost crashed. That wasn't like him. He was a careful man. He was never reckless. Never. He was angry with himself for losing control.

He drove toward the avenue. The traffic light was with him, and the nearest car was three or four blocks away, a lone pair of headlights dimmed and diffused by the falling snow. He turned the corner onto Lexington.

In three hundred feet, he came to the front of the

Bowerton Building. Ferns and flowers, molded in a twenty-foot-long rectangular bronze plaque, crowned the stonework above the four revolving doors. Part of the enormous lobby was visible beyond the entrance, and it appeared to be deserted. He drove near the curb, in the parking lane, barely moving, studying the building and the sidewalks and the calcimined street, looking for some sign of trouble and finding none.

Nevertheless, the plan had failed. Something had gone wrong in there. Terribly, terribly wrong.

Will Bollinger talk if he's caught? Billy wondered uneasily. Will he implicate me?

He would have to go to work without knowing how badly Dwight had failed, without knowing whether or not Bollinger would be – had been? – apprehended by the police. He was going to find it difficult to concentrate on his job tonight; but if he was going to construct an alibi to counter a possible confession from Dwight, it would help his case if he was calm tonight, as much like himself as he could be, as thorough and diligent as those who knew him expected him to be.

Franklin Dwight Bollinger was getting restless. He was bathed in a thin, oily sweat. His fingers ached from the tight grip he had kept on the Walther PPK. He'd been watching the stairwell exits for more than twenty minutes, but there was no sign of Harris or the woman.

Billy was gone by now, the schedule destroyed. Bollinger hoped he might salvage the plan. But at the same time he knew that wasn't possible. The situation had degenerated to this: slaughter them and get the hell out.

Where *is* Harris? he wondered. Has he sensed that I'm waiting here for him? Has he used his carnival act, his goddamned clairvoyance, to anticipate me?

He decided to wait five minutes more. Then he would be forced to go after them.

Staring out of the office window at an eerie panorama of gigantic, snow-swept buildings and fuzzy lights, Graham said, 'It's impossible.'

Beside him, Connie put one hand on his arm. '*Why* is it impossible?'

'It just is.'

'That's not good enough.'

'I can't climb it.'

'It's not a climb.'

'What?'

'It's a descent.'

'Doesn't matter.'

'Can it be done?'

'Not by me.'

'You climbed the ladder in the shaft.'

'That's different.'

'How?'

'Besides, you've never climbed.'

'You can teach me.'

'No.'

'Sure you can.'

'You can't learn on the sheer face of a forty-story building in the middle of a blizzard.'

'I'd have a damned good teacher,' she said.

'Oh, yeah. One who hasn't climbed in five years.'

'You still know how. You haven't forgotten.'

'I'm out of shape.'

'You're a strong man.'

'You forget my leg.'

She turned away from the window and went back to the door so that she could listen for Bollinger while she talked. 'Remember when Abercrombie and Fitch had a man scale their building to advertise a new line of climbing equipment?'

He didn't look away from the window. He was transfixed by the night. 'What about it?'

'At the time, you said what that man did wasn't really so difficult.'

'Did I?'

'You said a building, with all its ledges and setbacks, is an easy climb compared to almost any mountain.'

He said nothing. He remembered telling her that, and he knew he had been right. But when he'd said it he never thought he'd be called upon to *do* it. Images of Mount Everest and of hospital rooms filled his mind.

'This equipment you chose for the buyer's guide –'

'What about it?'

'It's the best, isn't it?'

'The best, or close to it.'

'We'd be perfectly outfitted.'

'If we try it, we'll die.'

'We'll die if we stay here.'

'Maybe not.'

'I think so. Absolutely.'

'There has to be an alternative.'

'I've outlined them already.'

'Maybe we *can* hide from him.'

'Where?'

'I don't know. But –'

'And we can't hide for seven hours.'

'This is crazy, dammit!'

'Can you think of anything better?'

'Give me time.'

'Bollinger will be here any minute.'

'The wind speed must be forty miles an hour at street level. At least when it's gusting. Fifty miles an hour up this high.'

'Will it blow us off?'

'We'd have to fight it every inch.'

'Won't we anchor the ropes?'

He turned away from the window. 'Yes, but –'

'And won't we be wearing those?' She pointed to a pair of safety harnesses that lay atop the pile of equipment.

'It'll be damned cold out there, Connie.'

'We've got the down-lined jackets.'

'But we don't have quilted, insulated pants. You're wearing ordinary jeans. So am I. For all the good they'll do us, we might as well be naked below the waist.'

'I can stand the cold.'

'Not for very long. Not cold as bitter as that.'

'How long will it take us to get to the street?'

'I don't know.'

'You must have *some* idea.'

'An hour. Maybe two hours.'

'That long?'

'You're a novice.'

'Couldn't we rappel?'

'Rappel?' He was appalled.

'It looks so easy. Swinging out and back, dropping a few feet with every swing, bouncing off the stone, dancing along the side of the building . . .'

'It looks easy, but it isn't.'

'But it's fast.'

'Jesus! You've never climbed before, and you want to rappel down.'

'I've got guts.'

'But no common sense.'

'Okay,' she said. 'We don't rappel.'

'We definitely don't rappel.'

'We go slow and easy.'

'We don't go at all.'

Ignoring him, she said, 'I can take two hours of the cold. I know I can. And if we keep moving, maybe it won't bother us so much.'

'We'll freeze to death.' He refused to be shaken from that opinion.

'Graham, we have a simple choice. Go or stay. If we make the climb, *maybe* we'll fall or freeze to death. If we stay here, we'll sure as hell be killed.'

'I'm not convinced it *is* that simple.'

'Yes, you are.'

He closed his eyes. He was furious with himself, sick of his inability to accept unpleasant realities, to risk pain, and to come face to face with his own fear. The climb would be dangerous. Supremely dangerous. It might even prove to be sheer folly; they could die in the first few minutes of the descent. But she was correct when she said they had no choice but to try it.

'Graham? We're wasting time.'

'You know the real reason why the climb isn't possible.'

'No,' she said. 'Tell me.'

He felt color and warmth come into his face. 'Connie, you aren't leaving me with any dignity.'

'I never took that from you. You've taken it from yourself.' Her lovely face was lined with sorrow. He could see that it hurt her to have to speak to him so bluntly. She came across the room, put one hand to his face. 'You've surrendered your dignity and your self-respect. Piece by piece.' Her voice was low, almost a whisper; it wavered. 'I'm afraid for you, afraid that if you don't stop throwing it away, you'll have nothing left. Nothing.'

'Connie . . .' He wanted to cry. But he had no tears for Graham Harris. He knew precisely what he had done to himself. He had no pity; he *despised* the man he'd become. He felt that, deep inside, he had always been a coward, and that his fall on Mount Everest had given him an excuse to retreat into fear. Why else had he resisted going to a psychiatrist? Every one of his doctors had suggested psychoanalysis. He suspected that he was comfortable in his fear; and that possibility sickened him. 'I'm afraid of my own shadow. I'd be no good to you out there.'

'You're not so frightened today as you were yesterday,' she said tenderly. 'Tonight, you've coped damned well. What about the elevator shaft? This morning, the thought of going down that ladder would have overwhelmed you.'

He was trembling.

'This is your chance,' she said. 'You can overcome the fear. I know you can.'

He licked his lips nervously. He went to the pile of gear in front of the photographic backdrop. 'I wish I could be half as sure of me as you are.'

Following him, she said, 'I understand what I'm asking of you. I know it'll be the hardest thing you've ever done.'

He remembered the fall vividly. He could close his eyes any time – even in a crowded room – and experience it again: his foot slipping, pain in the chest as the safety harness tightened around him, pain abruptly relieved as the rope snapped, breath caught like an unchewed lump of meat in his throat, then floating and floating and floating. The fall was only three hundred feet, and it had ended in a thick cushion of snow; it had seemed a mile.

She said, 'If you stay here, you'll die; but it'll be an easier death. The instant Bollinger sees you, he'll shoot to kill. He won't hesitate. It'll be over within a second for you.' She took hold of his hand. 'But it won't be like that for me.'

He looked up from the equipment. Her gray eyes radiated a fear as primal and paralyzing as his own.

'Bollinger will use me,' she said.

He was unable to speak.

'He'll cut me,' she said.

Unbidden, an image of Edna Mowry came to him. She had been holding her own bloody navel in her hand.

'He'll disfigure me.'

'Maybe –'

'He's the Butcher. Don't forget. Don't forget who he is. What he is.'

'God help me,' he said.

'I don't want to die. But if I *have* to die, I don't want it to be like that.' She shuddered. 'If we're not going to make the climb, if we're just going to wait for him here, then I want you to kill me. Hit me across the back of the head with something. Hit me very hard.'

Amazed, he said, 'What are you talking about?'

'Kill me before Bollinger can get to me. Graham, you owe me that much. You've got to do it.'

'I love you,' he said weakly. 'You're everything. There's nothing else for me.'

She was somber, a mourner at her own execution. 'If you love me, then you understand why you've got to kill me.'

'I couldn't do it.'

'We don't have much time,' she said. 'Either we get ready for the climb right now – or you kill me. Bollinger will be here any minute.'

Glancing at the main entrance to see if anyone was trying to get in, Bollinger crossed the marble floor and opened the white door. He stood at the bottom of the north stairs and listened for footsteps. There were none. No footsteps, no voices, no noise at all. He peered up the narrow, open core of the shaft, but he didn't see anyone moving alongside the switchback railing.

He went to the south stairs.

Those too were deserted.

He looked at his watch. 10:38.

Running some of Blake's verses through his mind to calm himself, he went to the elevator.

Well-made boots are [illegible]
They should be free [illegible]
from the best grade of [illegible]
preferably in [illegible]
Most important of [illegible]
stiff, with [illegible]
Graham was [illegible]
They were a perfect [illegible]
wear. Although [illegible]
brought him [illegible]
terror, he found [illegible]
reassuring. His [illegible]
ing gear [illegible]
against which [illegible]
terrie; test [illegible]
shown.

Both pairs of boots [illegible]
four sizes too large for [illegible]
either of them. If she [illegible]
and along the sides, she would [illegible]
wearing blocks of concrete [illegible]
misstep at some crucial point [illegible]

Fortunately, they found a pair [illegible]
that fitted well enough. The [illegible]

31

Well-made boots are essential to a serious climber. They should be five to seven inches high, crafted from the best grade of leather, lined with leather, preferably hand-sewn, with foam-padded tongues. Most important of all, the soles should be hard and stiff, with tough lugs made of Vibram.

Graham was wearing just such a pair of boots. They were a perfect fit, more like gloves than footwear. Although putting them on and lacing them up brought him closer to the act that he regarded with terror, he found the boots strangely comforting, reassuring. His familiarity with them, with climbing gear in general, seemed like a touchstone against which he could test for the old Graham Harris, test for a trace of the courage he'd once shown.

Both pairs of boots in the pile of equipment were four sizes too large for Connie. She couldn't wear either of them. If she stuffed paper into the toes and along the sides, she would feel as if she were wearing blocks of concrete; and she would surely misstep at some crucial point in the climb.

Fortunately, they found a pair of klettershoes that fitted well enough. The klettershoe - an anglicization of *Kletterschuh*, German for 'climbing shoe' – was lighter, tighter, more flexible, and not so high as standard climbing boots. The sole was of rubber, and the welt did not protrude, making it possible for the wearer to gain toeholds on even the narrowest ledges.

Although they would have to serve for want of something better, the klettershoes weren't suited for the climb that lay ahead. Because they were made of suede and were not waterproof, they should be used only in the fairest weather, never in a snowstorm.

To protect her feet from becoming wet and from the inevitable frostbite, Connie wore both socks and plastic binding. The socks were thick, gray, woolen; they came to mid-calf. The plastic was ordinarily used to seal up the dry food that a climber carried in his rucksack. Graham had wrapped her feet in two sheets of plastic, securing the waterproof material at her ankles with rubber bands.

They were both wearing heavy, bright red nylon parkas with hoods that tied under the chin. Between the outer nylon surface and the inner nylon lining, his jacket was filled with man-made insulation, sufficient for autumn climbing but not for the cold that awaited them tonight. Her parka was much better – although he hadn't explained that to her for fear she would insist that *he* wear it – because it was insulated with one hundred percent goose down. That made it the warmest garment, for its size and weight, that she could have worn.

Over the parka, each of them was wearing a *Klettergürtel*, a climbing harness, for protection in the event of a fall. This piece of equipment was a great improvement over the waistband that climbers had once used, for in a fall the band sometimes jerked so tight that it damaged the heart and lungs. The simple leather harness distributed the pressure over the entire body trunk, reducing the risk of a severe injury and virtually guaranteeing the climber that he would not turn upside down.

Connie was impressed by the *Klettergürtel*. As he strapped her into it, she said. 'It's perfect insurance, isn't it? Even if you fall, it brings you up short.'

Of course, if she didn't just slip or misplace her foot, if instead the rope broke, and if she was on a single line, the harness would not stop her fall. However, Connie didn't have to worry about that, for he was taking extraordinary safety measures with her: she would be going down on two independent lines. In addition to the main rope, he intended to fix her to a second which he would belay all the way to the street.

He would not be so well looked after as she was. There was no one to belay him. He would be descending last – on a single line.

He didn't explain that to her. When she got outside, the less she had to worry about, the better her chances were of coming out of this alive. Tension was good for a climber; but too much tension could cause him to make mistakes.

Both harnesses had accessory loops at the waist. Graham was carrying pitons, carabiners, expansion bolts, a hammer, and a compact battery-powered drill the size of two packs of cigarettes. In her harness loops, Connie had a variety of extra pitons and carabiners.

Besides the equipment hung on their harnesses, they were both burdened with rope. Connie had hundred-foot lengths of it at each hip; it was heavy, but so tightly coiled that it did not restrict her movements. Graham had another hundred-foot coil at his right hip. They were left with two shorter lengths: and these they would use for the first leg of the descent.

Last of all, they put on their gloves.

At every floor, Bollinger got off the elevator. If the entire level was occupied by one business firm, he tried the locked doors at opposite ends of the alcove. If it was an 'open' floor, he stepped out of the alcove to make certain there was no one in the corridor.

At every fifth floor, he looked not only into the corridor but into the stairs and the elevator shafts as well. On the first twenty floors, four elevator shafts served the building; from the twentieth to the thirty-fifth floors, two shafts; and from the thirty-fifth to the forty-second, only one shaft. In the first half of his vertical search, he wasted far more time than he could afford, opening the emergency doors to all of those shafts.

At ten-fifty he was on the fifteenth floor.

He had not found a sign of them. He was beginning to wonder if he was conducting the search properly. However, at the moment he was unable to see any other way to go about it.

He went to the sixteenth floor.

Connie pulled on the heavy cord and drew back the office draperies.

Graham unlatched the center window. The two

rectangular panes wouldn't budge at first, then abruptly gave with a squeal, opened inward like casement windows.

Wind exploded into the room. It had the voice of a living creature; its screams were piercing, demonic. Snowflakes swirled around him, danced across the top of the conference table and melted on its polished surface, beaded like dew on the grass-green carpet.

Leaning over the sill, he looked down the side of the Bowerton Building. The top five floors – and the four-story decorative pinnacle above them – were set back two yards from the bottom thirty-seven levels. Just three floors below, there was a six-foot-wide ledge that ringed the structure. The lower four-fifths of the building's face lay beyond the ledge, out of his line of sight.

The snow was falling so thickly that he could barely see the street lamps on the far side of Lexington Avenue. Under the lights, not even a small patch of pavement was visible.

In the few seconds he needed to survey the situation, the wind battered his head, chilled and numbed his exposed face.

'That's damned cold!' As he spoke, breath pluming out of him, he turned from the window. 'We're bound to suffer at least *some* frostbite.'

'We've got to go anyway,' she said.

'I know. I'm not trying to back out.'

'Should we wrap our faces?'

'With what?'

'Scarves –'

'The wind would cut through any material we've got handy, then paste it to our faces so we'd have trouble breathing. Unfortunately, the magazine didn't recommend any face masks in that buyer's guide. Otherwise, we'd have exactly what we need.'

'Then what can we do?'

He had a sudden thought and went to his desk. He stripped off his bulky gloves. The center drawer contained evidence of the hypochondria that had been an ever-growing component of his fear: Anacin, aspirin, half a dozen cold remedies, tetracycline capsules, throat lozenges, a thermometer in its case . . . He picked up a small tube and showed it to her.

'Chap Stick?' she asked.

'Come here.'

She went to him. 'That stuff's for chapped lips. If we're going to be frostbitten, why worry about a little thing like chapped lips?'

He pulled the cap off the tube, twisted the base to bring up the waxy stick, and coated her entire face – forehead, temples, cheeks, nose, lips and chin. 'With even a thin shield of this, the wind will need more time to leech the warmth out of you. And it'll keep your skin supple. Loss of heat is two-thirds of the danger. But loss of moisture along with loss of heat is what causes severe frostbite. The moisture in bitterly cold air doesn't get to your skin; in fact, subzero wind can dry out your face almost as thoroughly as desert air.'

'I was right,' she said.

'Right about what?'

'There's some Nick Charles in you.'

At eleven o'clock, Bollinger entered the elevator, switched it on, and pressed the button for the twenty-second floor.

32

The window frame was extremely sturdy, not cold-pressed and not of aluminum as were most of the window frames in buildings erected during the past thirty years. The grooved, steel center post was almost an inch thick and appeared to be capable of supporting hundreds of pounds without bending or breaking loose from the sash.

Harris hooked a carabiner to the post.

This piece of hardware was one of the most important that a climber carried. Carabiners were made of steel or alloy and came in several shapes – oval D, offset D, and pear or keyhole – but the oval was used more often than any of the others. It was approximately three and a half inches by one and three-quarters inches, and it resembled nothing so much as an oversized key ring or perhaps an elongated chain link. A spring-loaded gate opened on one side of the oval, making it possible for the climber to connect the carabiner to the eye of a piton; he could also slip a loop of rope onto the metal ring. A carabiner, which was sometimes referred to as a 'snap link,' could be employed to join two ropes at any point along them, which was essential when the ends of those lines were secured above and below. A vital – but not the only – function of the highly polished snap links was to prevent ropes from chaffing each other, to guard against their fraying through on the rough, unpolished eye of a piton or on the sharp edge of a rock; carabiners saved lives.

At Graham's direction, Connie had stripped the manufacturer's plastic bands from an eighty-foot coil of red and blue hawser-laid nylon rope.

'It doesn't look strong,' she said.

'It's got a breaking strength of four thousand pounds.'

'So thin.'

'Seven-sixteenths of an inch.'

'I guess you know what you're doing.'

Smiling reassuringly, he said, 'Relax.'

He tied a knot in one end of the rope. That done, he grasped the double loop that sprouted above the knot and slipped it through the gate of the carabiner that was attached to the window post.

He was surprised at how quickly he was working, and by the ease with which he had fashioned the complex knot. He seemed to be operating on instinct more than on knowledge. In five years he had not forgotten anything.

'This will be your safety line,' he told her.

The carabiner was one of those that came with a metal sleeve that fitted over the gate to guard against an accidental opening. He screwed the sleeve in place.

He picked up the rope and pulled it through his hands, quickly measuring eleven yards of it. He took a folding knife from a pocket of his parka and cut the rope, dropped one piece to the floor. He tied the cut end of the shorter section to her harness, so that she was attached to the window post by a thirty-foot umbilical. He took one end of the other piece of rope and tied it around her waist, using a bowline knot.

Patting the windowsill, he said, 'Sit up here.'

She sat facing him, her back to the wind and snow.

He pushed the thirty-foot rope out of the window; and the loop of slack, from the post to Connie's harness, swung in the wind. He arranged the forty-five-foot length on the office floor, carefully coiled it to be certain that it would pay out without tangling, and finally tied the free end around his waist.

He intended to perform a standing hip belay. On a mountain, it was always possible that a belayer might be jerked from his standing position if he was not anchored by another rope and a well-placed piton; he could lose his balance and fall, along with the person whom he was belaying. Therefore, a standing belay was considered less desirable than one accomplished from a sitting position. However, because Connie weighed sixty pounds less than he, and because the window was waist high, he didn't think she would be able to drag him out of the room.

Standing with his legs spread to improve his balance, he picked up the forty-five-foot line at a point midway between the neatly piled coil and Connie. He had knotted the rope at his navel; now, he passed it behind him and across the hips at the belt line. The rope that came from Connie went around his left hip and then around his right; therefore, his left hand was the guide hand, while the right was the braking hand.

From his anchor point six feet in front of her, he said, 'Ready'?'

She bit her lip.

'The ledge is only thirty feet below.'

'Not so far,' she said weakly.

'You'll be there before you know it.'

She forced a smile.

She looked down at her harness and tugged on it, as if she thought it might have come undone.

'Remember what to do?' he asked.

'Hold the line with both hands above my head. Don't try to help. Look for the ledge, get my feet on it right away, don't let myself be lowered past it.'

'And when you get there?'

'First, I untie myself.'

'But only from this line.'

'Yes.'

'Not from the other.'

She nodded.

'Then, when you've untied yourself –'

'I jerk on this line twice.'

'That's right. I'll put you down as gently as I can.'

In spite of the stinging cold wind that whistled through the open window on both sides of her, her face was pale. 'I love you,' she said.

'And I love you.'

'You can do this.'

'I hope so.'

'I *know*.'

His heart was pounding.

'I trust you,' she said.

He realized that if he allowed her to die during the climb, he would have no right or reason to save himself. Life without her would be an unbearable passage through guilt and loneliness, a gray emptiness worse than death. If she fell, he might as well pitch himself after her.

He was scared.

All he could do was repeat what he had already said, 'I love you.'

Taking a deep breath, leaning backward, she said, 'Well . . . woman overboard!'

The corridor was dark and deserted.

Bollinger returned to the elevator and pressed the button for the twenty-seventh floor.

The instant that [illegible] windowsill she sensed the [illegible] space beneath her. [illegible] be profoundly affected [illegible] She was even [illegible] expected to be. The [illegible] mental impact on her [illegible] found it hard to breathe [illegible] her pulse rate soar [illegible] stomach contracted [illegible]

She resisted the [illegible] before it was [illegible] reached [illegible] hands.

The wind [illegible] her face and stung the [illegible] around her eyes.

In order to see at all [illegible] peer out through the [illegible] slits. Otherwise, the windowsill [illegible] with her own tears. [illegible] climbing equipment in the [illegible] had not contained snow goggles.

She glanced down at the [illegible]

33

The instant that Connie slipped backward off the windowsill she sensed the hundreds of feet of open space beneath her. She didn't need to look down to be profoundly affected by that great, dark gulf. She was even more terrified than she had expected to be. The fear had a physical as well as a mental impact on her. Her throat constricted; she found it hard to breathe. Her chest felt tight, and her pulse rate soared. Suddenly acidic, her stomach contracted sickeningly.

She resisted the urge to clutch the windowsill before it was out of her grasp. Instead, she reached overhead and gripped the rope with both hands.

The wind rocked her from side to side. It pinched her face and stung the thin rim of ungreased skin around her eyes.

In order to see at all, she was forced to squint, to peer out through the narrowest of lash-shielded slits. Otherwise, the wind would have blinded her with her own tears. Unfortunately, the pile of climbing equipment in the art director's office had not contained snow goggles.

She glanced down at the ledge toward which she

was slowly moving. It was six feet wide, but to her it looked like a tightrope.

His feet slipped on the carpet.

He dug in his heels.

Judging by the amount of rope still coiled beside him, she was not even halfway to the ledge. Yet he felt as if he had lowered her at least a hundred feet.

Initially, the strain on Graham's arms and shoulders had been tolerable. But as he payed out the line, he became increasingly aware of the toll taken by five years of inactivity. With each foot of rope, new aches sprang up like sparks in his muscles, spread toward each other, fanned into cracking fires.

Nevertheless, the pain was the least of his worries. More important, he was facing away from the office doors. And he could not forget the vision: a bullet in the back, blood, and then darkness.

Where was Bollinger?

The farther Connie descended, the less slack there was in the line that connected her to the window post. She hoped that Graham had estimated its length correctly. If not, she might be in serious trouble. A too-long safety line posed no threat; but if it was too short, she would be hung up a foot or two from the ledge. She would have to climb back to the window so that Graham could rectify the situation – or she would have to give up the safety line altogether, proceed to the setback on just the belayer's rope. Anxiously, she watched the safety line as it gradually grew taut.

Overhead, the main rope was twisting and

untwisting with lateral tension. As the thousands of nylon strands repeatedly tightened, relaxed, tightened, she found herself turning slowly in a semicircle from left to right and back again. This movement was in addition to the pendulumlike swing caused by the wind; and of course it made her increasingly ill.

She wondered if the rope would break. Surely, all of that twisting and untwisting began where the rope dropped away from the window. Was the thin line even now fraying at its contact point with the sill?

Graham had said there would be some dangerous friction at the sill. But he had assured her that she would be on the ledge before the nylon fibers had even been slightly bruised. Nylon was tough material. Strong. Reliable. It would not wear through from a few minutes - or even a quarter-hour - of heavy friction.

Still, she wondered.

At eight minutes after eleven, Frank Bollinger started to search the thirtieth floor.

He was beginning to feel that he was trapped in a surreal landscape of doors; hundreds upon hundreds of doors. All night long he had been opening them, anticipating sudden violence, overflowing with that tension that made him feel *alive*. But all of the doors opened on the same thing: darkness, emptiness, silence. Each door promised to deliver what he had been hunting for, but not one of them kept the promise.

It seemed to him that the wilderness of doors was a condition not merely of this one night but of his entire life. Doors. Doors that opened on darkness. On emptiness. On blind passages and dead ends of every sort. Each day of his life, he had expected to find a door that, when flung wide, would present him with all that he deserved. Yet that golden door eluded him. He had not been treated fairly. After all, he was one of the new men, superior to everyone he saw around him. Yet what had he become in thirty-seven years? Anything? Not a president. Not even a senator. Not famous. Not rich. He was nothing but a lousy vice detective, a cop whose working life was spent in the grimy subculture of whores, pimps, gamblers, addicts and petty racketeers.

That was why Harris (and tens of millions like him) had to die. They were subhumans, vastly inferior to the new breed of men. Yet for every new man, there were a million old ones. Because there was strength in numbers, these pitiful creatures – risking thermonuclear destruction to satisfy their greed and their fondness for childish posturing – held on to the world's power, money and resources. Only through the greatest slaughter in history, only in the midst of Armageddon, could the new men seize what was rightfully theirs.

The thirtieth level was deserted, as were the stairs and the elevator shafts.

He went up one floor.

Connie's feet touched the ledge. Thanks to the scouring wind, the stone was pretty much free of snow; therefore, there had been no chance for the snow to be pressed into ice. She wasn't in any danger of sliding off her perch.

She put her back to the face of the building, staying as far from the brink as she could.

Surprisingly, with stone under her feet, she was more impressed by the gulf in front of her than when she was dangling in empty space. Swinging at the end of the rope, she had not been able to see the void in the proper perspective. Now, with the benefit of secure footing, she found the thirty-eight-story drop doubly terrifying; it seemed a bottomless pit.

She untied the knot at her harness, freed herself of the main line. She jerked on the rope twice, hard.

Immediately Graham reeled it up.

In a minute he would be on his way to her.

Would he panic when he got out here?

I trust him, she told herself. I really do. I *have* to.

Nonetheless, she was afraid he would get only part of the way out of the window before he turned and fled, leaving her stranded.

Graham took off his gloves [illegible] window, and left the [illegible] planed granite [illegible] ages. However, before [illegible] fingertips, he discovered [illegible] that suited his purpose [illegible]

Keeping one hand [illegible] lose it, he took the [illegible] tool straps at his waist. [illegible] ing out as far as he [illegible] the steel peg into the [illegible]

The light he had to [illegible] It came from the [illegible] the decorative [illegible] feet above him. [illegible] white.

From his upside-down position [illegible] more slowly than he would have [illegible] finished at last, he looked over his shoulder [illegible] Bollinger was behind him. [illegible]

The piton felt as if it were well placed [illegible] good grip on it, tried to wiggle it. It was firm.

He snapped a carabiner through [illegible] the piton.

34

Graham took off his gloves, leaned out of the window, and felt the stone below the sash. It was planed granite, a rock meant to withstand the ages. However, before the icy wind could numb his fingertips, he discovered a tiny horizontal fissure that suited his purpose.

Keeping one hand on the crack in order not to lose it, he took the hammer and a piton from the tool straps at his waist. Balanced on the sill, leaning out as far as he dared, he put the sharp tip of the steel peg into the crack and pounded it home.

The light he had to work by was barely adequate. It came from the aircraft warning lights that ringed the decorative pinnacle of the building just thirty feet above him; it alternated between red and white.

From his upside-down position, the work went more slowly than he would have liked. When he finished at last, he looked over his shoulder to see if Bollinger was behind him. He was still alone.

The piton felt as if it were well placed. He got a good grip on it, tried to wiggle it. It was firm.

He snapped a carabiner through the eye of the piton.

He snapped another carabiner to the center post of the window, above the one that secured Connie's safety line.

Next, he pulled the knots out of the belaying rope. He took it from around his waist and dropped it on the floor by the window.

He closed one of the tall, rectangular panes as best he could; the carabiners fixed to the center post would not permit it to close all the way. He would attempt to shut the other half of the window from the outside.

He hurried to the draw cords and pulled the green velvet drapes into place.

Eventually, Bollinger would come back to this office and would realize that they had gone out of the window. But Graham wanted to conceal the evidence of their escape as long as possible.

Stepping behind the drapes, he sidled along to the window. Wind roared through the open pane and billowed the velvet around him.

He picked up an eleven-yard line that he had cut from another hundred-foot coil. He tied it to his harness and to the free carabiner on the window post. There was no one here to belay him as he had done Connie, but he had worked out a way to avoid a single-line descent; he would have a safety tether exactly like Connie's.

He quickly tied a figure-eight knot in one end of the forty-five-foot-line. Leaning out of the window once more, he hooked the double loops of rope through the carabiner that was linked to the piton. Then he screwed the sleeve over the gate, locking the snap link. He tossed the rope into the night and watched to be sure that it hung straight and unobstructed from the piton. This would be his rappelling line.

He was not adhering strictly to orthodox mountain climbing procedure. But then this 'mountain' certainly was not orthodox either. The situation called for flexibility, for a few original methods.

After he had put on his gloves again, he took hold of the thirty-foot safety line. He wrapped it once around his right wrist and then seized it tightly with the same hand. Approximately four feet of rope lay between his hand and the anchor point on the window post. In the first few seconds after he went through the window, he would be hanging by his right arm, four feet under the sill.

He got on his knees on the window ledge, facing the lining of the office drapes. Slowly, cautiously, reluctantly, he went out of the room backward, feet first. Just before he overbalanced and slid all the way out, he closed the open half of the window as far as the carabiners would allow. Then he dropped four feet.

Memories of Mount Everest burst upon him, clamored for his attention. He shoved them down, desperately forced them deep into his mind.

He tasted vomit at the back of his mouth. But he swallowed hard, swallowed repeatedly until his throat was clear. He *willed* himself not to be sick, and it worked. At least for the moment.

With his left hand he plucked the rappelling line from the face of the building. Holding that loosely, he reached above his head and grabbed the safety rope that he already had in his right hand. Both hands on the shorter line, he raised his knees in a fetal position and planted his boots against the granite. Pulling hand over hand on the safety tether, he took three small steps up the sheer wall until he was balanced against the building at a forty-five-degree angle. The toes of his boots were jammed into a narrow mortar seam with all the force he could apply.

Satisfied with his precarious position, he let go of the safety tether with his left hand.

Although he remained securely anchored, the very act of letting go of anything at that height made the vomit rise in his throat once more. He gagged, held it down, quickly recovered.

He was balanced on four points: his right hand on the shorter rope, now only two feet from the window post; his left hand on the line with which he would rappel down; his right foot; his left foot. He clung like a fly to the side of the highrise.

Keeping his eyes on the piton that thrust up between his spread feet, he jerked on the rapelling line several times. Hard. The piton didn't move. He shifted his weight to the longer line but kept his right-hand grip on the safety tether. Even with a hundred and fifty pounds of downward drag, the piton did not shift in the crack.

Convinced that the peg was well placed, he released the safety tether.

Now he was balanced on three points: left hand on the long line, both feet on the wall, still at a forty-five-degree angle to the building.

Although he would not be touching it again before he reached the ledge, the safety rope would nevertheless bring him up short of death if the longer line broke while he was rappelling down to Connie.

He told himself to remember that. Remember and stave off panic. Panic was the real enemy. It could kill him faster than Bollinger could. The tether was there. Linking his harness to the window post. He must remember . . .

With his free hand, he groped under his thigh, felt behind himself for the long rope that he already held in his other hand. After a maddening few seconds, he found it. Now, the line on which he would rappel came from the piton to his left hand in front of him, passed between his legs at crotch level to his right hand behind him. With that hand he brought the rope forward, over his right hip, across his chest, over his head, and finally over his left shoulder. It hung down his back, passed through his right hand, and ran on into empty space.

He was perfectly positioned.

The left hand was his guiding hand.

The right hand was his braking hand.

He was ready to rappel.

For the first time since he had come through the window, he took a good look around him. Dark monoliths, gigantic skyscrapers rose eerily out of the winter storm. Hundreds of thousands of points of light, made hazy and even more distant by the falling snow, marked the night on every side of him. Manhattan to his left. Manhattan to his right. Manhattan behind him. Most important – Manhattan *below* him. Six hundred feet of empty night waiting to swallow him. Strangely, for an instant he felt as if this were a miniature replica of the city, a tiny reproduction that was forever frozen in plastic; he felt as if he were also tiny, as if he were suspended in a paperweight, one of those clear hemispheres that filled with artificial snow when it was shaken. As unexpectedly as it came, the illusion passed: the city became huge again; the concrete canyon below appeared to be bottomless; however, while all else returned to normal, he remained tiny, insignificant.

When he first came out of the window, he had focused his attention on pitons, ropes and technical maneuvers. Thus occupied, he had been able to ignore his surroundings, to blunt his awareness of them.

That was no longer possible. Suddenly, he was *too* aware of the city and of how far it was to the street.

Inevitably, such awareness brought unwanted memories: *his foot slipping, harness jerking tight, rope snapping, floating, floating, floating, floating, striking, darkness, splinters of pain in his legs, darkness again, a hot iron in his guts, pain breaking like glass in his back, blood, darkness, hospital rooms. . . .*

Although the bitterly cold wind pummeled his face, sweat popped out on his brow and along his temples.

He was trembling.

He knew he couldn't make the climb.

Floating, floating . . .

He couldn't move at all.

Not an inch.

In the elevator, Bollinger hesitated. He was about to press the button for the twenty-third floor, when he realized that, after he lost track of them, Harris and the woman apparently had not continued down toward the lobby. They had vanished on the twenty-seventh level. He had searched that floor and all those below it; and he was as certain as he could be, short of shooting open every locked door, that they were not in the lower three-fourths of the building. They'd gone up. Back to Harris's office? As soon as that occurred to him, he knew it was true, and he knew why they had done it. They'd gone up because that was the last thing he would expect them to do. If they had continued down the stairs or elevator shaft, he would have nailed them in minutes. Sure as hell. But, in going up, they had confused him and gained time.

Forty-five minutes of time, he thought angrily. That bastard has made a fool out of me. Forty-five minutes. But not one goddamned minute more.

He pushed the button for the fortieth floor.

Six hundred feet.

Twice as far as he had fallen on Everest.

And this time there would be no miracle to save him, no deep snowdrift to cushion the impact. He would be a bloody mess when the police found him. Broken. Ruined. Lifeless.

Although he could see nothing of it, he stared intently at the street. The darkness and snow obscured the pavement. Yet he could not look away. He was mesmerized not by what he saw, but by what he didn't *need* to see, transfixed by what he *knew* lay below the night and below the shifting white curtains of the storm.

He closed his eyes. Thought about courage. Thought about how far he had come. Toes pressed into the shallow mortar-filled groove between two blocks of granite. Left hand in front. Right hand behind. Ready, get set . . . but he couldn't go.

When he opened his eyes, he saw Connie on the ledge.

She motioned for him to hurry.

If he didn't move, she would die. He would fail her utterly. She didn't deserve that after the eighteen months she'd given him, eighteen months of tender care and saintlike understanding. She hadn't once criticized him for whining, for his paranoia or his self-pity or his selfishness. She had put herself in emotional jeopardy that was no less terrifying than the physical risk demanded of him. He knew that mental anguish was every bit as painful as a broken leg. In return for those eighteen months, he had to make this climb for her. He owed her that much; hell, he owed her *everything*.

The perspiration had dissolved some of the coating of Chap Stick on his forehead and cheeks. As the wind dried the sweat, it chilled his face. He realized again how little time they could spend out here before the winter night sapped their strength.

He looked up at the piton that anchored him.

Connie will die if you don't do this.

He was squeezing the line too tightly with his left hand, which ought to be used only to guide him. He should hold the line *loosely*, using his right hand to pass rope and to brake.

Connie will die . . .

He relaxed his left-hand grip.

He told himself not to look down. Took a deep breath. Let it out. Started to count to ten. Told himself he was stalling. Pushed off the wall.

Don't panic!

As he swung backward into the night, he slid down the rope. When he glided back to the wall, both feet in front of him and firmly planted against the granite, pain zigzagged through his game leg. He winced, but he knew he could bear it. When he looked down, he saw that he had descended no more than two feet: but the fact that he had gotten anywhere at all made the pain seem unimportant.

He had intended to thrust away from the stone

with all his strength and to cover two yards on each long arc. But he could not do it. Not yet. He was too scared to rappel as enthusiastically as he had done in the past; furthermore, a more vigorous descent would make the pain in his leg unbearable.

Instead, he pushed from the wall again, swung backward, dropped two feet along the line, swooped back to the wall. And again: just a foot or eighteen inches this time. Little mincing steps. A cautious dance of fear along the face of the building. Out, down, in; out, down, in; out, down, in . . .

The terror had not evaporated. It was in him yet, bubbling, thick as stew. A cancer that had fed upon him and grown for years was not likely to vanish through natural remission in a few minutes. However, he was no longer overwhelmed by fear, incapacitated by it. He could see ahead to a day when he might be cured of it; and that was a fine vision.

When he finally dared to look down, he saw that he was so near the ledge that he no longer needed to rappel. He let go of the rope and dropped the last few feet.

Connie pressed close to him. She had to shout to be heard above the wind. 'You did it.'

'I did it!'

'You've beaten it.'

'So far.'

'Maybe this is far enough.'

'What?'

She pointed to the window beside them. 'What if we break in here?'

'Why should we?'

'It's somebody's office. We could hide in it.'

'What about Bollinger?'

She raised her voice a notch to compensate for a new gust of wind. 'Sooner or later, he'll go to your office.'

'So?'

'He'll see the window. Carabiners and ropes.'

'I know.'

'He'll think we went all the way to the street.'

'Maybe he will. I doubt it.'

'Even if he doesn't think that, he won't know where we stopped. He can't blast open every door in the building, looking for us.'

The wind *whooshed* between them, rebounded from the building, rocked them as if they were toy figures. It wailed: a banshee.

Snowflakes sliced into Graham's eyes. They were so fine and cold that they affected him almost as grains of salt would have done. He squeezed his eyes shut, trying to force out the sudden pain. He had some success; but the pain was replaced by a copious flow of tears that temporarily blinded him.

They pressed their foreheads together, trying to get closer so they wouldn't have to yell at each other.

'We can hide until people come to work,' she said.

'Tomorrow's Saturday.'

'*Some* people will work. The custodial crews, at least.'

'The city will be paralyzed by morning,' he said. 'This is a blizzard! No one will go to work.'

'Then we hide until Monday.'

'What about water? Food?'

'A big office will have water coolers. Coffee and soda-vending machines. Maybe even a candy and cracker vendor.'

'Until Monday?'

'If we have to.'

'That's a long time.'

She jerked one hand to the void at her left side 'And that's a long *climb!*'

'Agreed.'

'Come on,' she said impatiently. 'Let's smash in the window.'

Bollinger stepped over the fallen liquor cabinet and looked around Harris's office.

Nothing out of the ordinary. No sign of the prey.

Where in the name of God *were* they?

He was turning to leave when the green velvet drapes billowed out from the wall.

He brought up the Walther PPK, almost opened fire.

Before he could squeeze off the first shot, the drapes fell back against the wall. Nobody could be hiding behind them; there wasn't enough room for that.

He went to one end of the drapes and found the draw cords. The green velvet folded back on itself with a soft hiss.

As soon as the middle window was revealed, he saw that something was wrong with it. He went to it and opened the tall, rectangular panes.

The wind rushed in at him, fluttered his unbuttoned collar, mussed his hair, moaned to him. Hard-driven flakes of snow peppered his face.

He saw the carabiners on the center post, and the ropes leading from them.

He leaned out of the window, looked down the side of the building.

'I'll be damned!' he said.

Graham was trying to unhook the hammer from

the accessory strap on his safety harness, but he was hampered by his heavy gloves. Without the gloves, it would have been an easy chore, but he didn't want to take them off out here for fear they would slip away from him and disappear over the edge. If something went wrong and they were forced to continue the climb, he would need gloves desperately.

Above him, the wind made a strange sound. *Whump!* A loud, blunt noise. Like a muffled crack of thunder.

He finally got the hammer off the strap.

Whump!

Connie grabbed his arm. 'Bollinger!'

At first he didn't know what she meant. He looked up only because she did.

Thirty feet above them, Bollinger was leaning out of the window.

To Connie, Graham said, 'Stand against the wall!'

She didn't move. She seemed stunned. This was the first time she had ever *looked* frightened.

'Don't make a target of yourself!' he shouted.

She pressed her back to the building.

'Untie yourself from the safety line,' he said.

Overhead, a tongue of flame licked out of the pistol's muzzle: *whump!*

Graham swung the hammer, struck the window.

Glass exploded inward.

Frantically, unable to forget the vision of himself being shot in the back, he smashed the stubborn, jagged shards that clung to the frame.

Whump!

The sharp sound of a ricochet made Graham jump. The bullet skipped off the stone inches from his face.

He was sweating again.

Bollinger shouted something.

The wind tore his words apart, transformed them into meaningless sounds.

Graham didn't look up. He kept working at the spiked edges of the window.

Whump!

'Go!' he shouted as he shattered the last dangerous piece of glass.

Connie scrambled over the windowsill, disappeared into the dark office.

He slipped the safety line knot at his harness.

Whump!

The shot was so close that he cried out involuntarily. The slug plucked at the sleeve of his parka. He was unbalanced by the surprise, and for an instant he thought he would fall off the ledge.

Whump!

Whump!

He plunged forward, through the broken window, expecting to be stopped at the last second by a bullet in the spine.

35

In the unlighted office on the thirty-eighth floor, the glass crunched under their feet.

Connie said, 'How could he miss us?'

As he patted the sweat from his face with the palm of his glove, Graham said, 'Wind's near gale force. Could have deflected the bullets slightly.'

'In just thirty feet?'

'Maybe. Besides, he was firing from a bad angle. Leaning out the window, shooting down and in. Light was bad. Wind was in his face. He'd have been damned lucky if he'd hit us.'

'We can't stay here as we planned,' she said.

'Of course not. He knows which floor we're on. He's probably running for the elevator right now.'

'We go back out?'

'I sure don't want to.'

'He'll keep popping up along the way, trying to shoot us off the side of the building.'

'Do we have a choice?'

'None,' she said. 'Ready to climb?'

'As I'll ever be.'

'You've done well.'

'I'm not all the way down yet.'

'You'll make it.'

when the climber left the rope, releasing the tension, and when the rope was tugged in the proper manner, the knot would slip open. He jerked on the line, then again, and a third time. Finally it freed itself from the snap link and tumbled down into his lap.

He took a folding knife from a pocket of his parka, opened it. He cut two five-foot pieces from the eleven-yard safety line, then put the knife away.

He stood up, tottering slightly as pain shimmered through his bad leg.

One of the five-foot lines was for him. He tied an end of it to his harness. He tied the other end to a carabiner and snapped the carabiner to the window post.

Leaning in the window, he said, 'Connie?'

She stepped out of the shadows, into the wan fan of light. 'I was listening.'

'Hear anything?'

'Not yet.'

'Come out here.'

He wished Billy could be here for the kill. He felt that Billy was half of him, fifty percent of his flesh and blood and mind. Without Billy, he wasn't fully alive at moments like this. Without Billy, he could experience only a part of the thrill, half of the excitement.

On his way to the elevator, Bollinger thought about Billy, mostly about the first few nights they had known each other.

They had met on a Friday and spent nine hours in a private all-night club on Forty-fourth Street. They had left well after dawn, and they were amazed at how the time had flown. The bar was a favorite hangout for city detectives and was always busy; however, it seemed to Bollinger that he and Billy had been the only people in the place, all alone in their corner booth.

From the start they weren't awkward with each other. He felt as if they were twin brothers, as if they shared that mythical oneness of twins in addition to years of daily contact. They talked rapidly, eagerly. No chitchat or gossip. Conversation. Honest-to-God conversation. It was an exchange of ideas and sentiments that Bollinger had never enjoyed with anyone else. Nothing was taboo. Politics. Religion. Poetry. Sex. Self-appraisal. They found a phenomenal number of things about which they held the same unorthodox opinions. After nine hours, they knew each other better than either of them had ever known another human being.

The following night they met at the bar, talked, drank, picked up a good-looking whore and took her to Billy's apartment. The three of them had gone to bed together, but not in a bisexual sense. In fact, it would be more accurate to say that the two of them had gone to bed with her, for although they performed, sometimes separately and sometimes simultaneously, a wide variety of sex acts with and upon her, Billy did not touch Bollinger, nor did Bollinger touch Billy.

That night, sex was more dynamic, exhilarating, frenzied, manic, and ultimately more exhausting than Bollinger had ever imagined it could be. Billy certainly didn't look like a stud. Far from it. But he was precisely that, insatiable. He delighted in withholding his orgasm for hours, for he knew that the longer he denied himself, the more shattering the climax when it finally came. A sensualist, he preferred to refuse immediate satisfaction in favor of a far greater series of sensations later on. Bollinger realized from the moment he climbed into the bed that he was being tested. Rated. Billy was watching. He found it difficult to match the pace set by the older man, but he did. Even the girl complained of being worn out, used up.

He vividly recalled the position in which he'd been when he'd climaxed, because afterward he suspected that Billy had maneuvered him into it. The girl was on hands and knees in the center of the bed. Billy knelt in front of her. Bollinger knelt behind, stroking her dog-fashion. He faced Billy across her back; later, he knew that Billy had wanted to finish while confronting him.

He watched himself moving in and out of the girl, then looked up and saw Billy staring at him. Staring intently. Eyes wide, electric. Eyes that weren't entirely sane. Although he was frightened by it, he returned the stare – and was plunged into an hallucinogenic experience. He imagined he was rising out of his body, felt as if he were floating toward Billy. And as he floated, he shrank until he was so small he could tumble into those eyes. Knowing that it was an illusion in no way detracted from the impact of it; he could have sworn that he actually *was* sinking into Billy's eyes, sinking down, down . . .

His climax was considerably more than a biological function; it joined him to the whore on a physical level, but it also tied him to Billy on a much higher plane. He spurted deep into her vagina, and precisely at that moment Billy spilled seed into her mouth. In the throes of an intense orgasm, Bollinger had the odd notion that he and Billy had grown incredibly inside of the girl, had swelled and lengthened until they were touching at the center of her. Then he went one step further, lost all awareness of the woman; so far as he was concerned, he and Billy were the only people in the room. In his mind he saw them standing with the tips of their organs pressed together, ejaculating into each other's penis. The image was powerful but strangely asexual. There was certainly nothing *homosexual* about it. Absolutely nothing. He wasn't queer. He had no doubt about that. None at all. The imaginary act that preoccupied him was similar to the ritual by which members of certain American Indian tribes had once become blood brothers. The Indians cut their hands and pressed the cuts together; because they believed that the blood flowed from the body of one into that of the other, they felt that they would be part of each other forever. Bollinger's bizarre vision was like the Indians' blood-brother ceremony. It was an oath, a most sacred bond. And he knew that a metamorphosis had taken place; henceforth, they were not two men but one.

Now, feeling incomplete without Billy beside him, he reached the elevator cab and switched it on.

Connie clambered through the window, onto the thirty-eighth-floor setback.

Graham quickly tied the free end of the hundred-foot main line to her harness.

'Ready?' she asked.

'Not quite.'

His hands were getting numb. His fingertips stung, and his knuckles ached as if they were arthritic.

He tied carabiners to both ends of one of the five-foot pieces of rope he had cut. He snapped both carabiners to a metal ring on her harness. The rope between them looped all the way to her knees.

He clipped the hammer to the accessory strap on the waist belt of her harness.

'What's all this for?' she asked.

'The next setback is five stories down. Looks about half as wide as this one. I'll lower you the same way I got you here. I'll be anchored to the window post.' He tugged on his own five-foot tether. 'But we don't have time to rig a seventy-five-foot safety line for you. You'll have to go on just a single rope.'

She chewed her lower lip, nodded.

'As soon as you reach that ledge,' Graham said, 'look for a narrow, horizontal masonry seam between blocks of granite. The narrower the better. But don't waste too much time comparing cracks. Use the hammer to pound in a piton.'

'This short rope you just hooked onto me: is that to be my safety line when I get down there?'

'Yes. Unclip one end of it from your harness and snap the carabiner to the piton. Make sure the sleeve is screwed over the gate.'

'Sleeve?'

He showed her what he meant. 'As soon as you've got the sleeve in place, untie yourself from the main line so that I can reel it up and use it.'

She gave him his gloves.

He put them on. 'One more thing. I'll be letting the rope out much faster than I did the first time. Don't panic. Just hold on, relax, and keep your eyes open for the ledge coming up under you.'

'All right.'

'Any questions?'

'No.'

She sat on the edge of the setback, dangled her legs over the gulf.

He picked up the rope, flexed his cold hands several times to be certain he had a firm grip. A meager trace of warmth had begun to seep into his fingers. He spread his feet, took a deep breath, and said, 'Go!'

She slid off the ledge, into empty space.

Pain pulsated through his arms and shoulders as her full weight suddenly dragged on him. Gritting his teeth, he payed out the rope as fast as he dared.

In the thirty-eighth-floor corridor, Frank Bollinger had some difficulty deciding which business lay directly under Harris's office. Finally, he settled on two possibilities: Boswell Patent Brokerage and Dentonwick Mail Order Sales.

Both doors were locked.

He pumped three bullets into the lock on the Dentonwick office. Pushed open the door. Fired twice into the darkness. Leaped inside, crouched, fumbled for the wall switch, turned on the overhead lights.

The first of the three rooms was deserted. He proceeded cautiously to search the other two.

The tension went out of the line.

Connie had reached the ledge five stories below.

Nevertheless, he kept his hands on the rope and was prepared to belay her again if she slipped and fell before she had anchored her safety tether.

He heard two muffled shots.

The fact that he could hear them at all above the howling wind meant that they were frighteningly close.

But what was Bollinger shooting at?

The office behind Graham remained dark; but suddenly, lights came on beyond the windows of the office next door.

Bollinger was too damned close.

Is this where it happens? he wondered. Is this where I get the bullet in the back?

Sooner than he had expected, the signal came on the line: two sharp tugs.

He reeled in the rope, wondering if he had as much as a minute left before Bollinger found the correct office, the broken window – and him.

If he was going to reach that ledge five stories below before Bollinger had a chance to kill him, he would have to rappel much faster than he had done the first time.

Once more, the rope passed over regularly spaced windows. He would have to be careful not to put his feet through one of them. Because he'd have to take big steps rather than little ones, and because he'd have to descend farther on each arc and take less time to calculate his movements, avoiding the glass would be far more difficult than it had been from the fortieth to the thirty-eighth floor.

His prospects rekindled his terror. Perhaps it was fortunate that he needed to hurry. If he'd had time to delay, the fear might have grown strong enough to immobilize him again.

Harris and the woman were not in the offices of Dentonwick Mail Order Sales.

Bollinger returned to the corridor. He fired two shots into the door of the Boswell Patent Brokerage suite.

36

Boswell Patent Brokerage occupied three small rooms, all of them shabbily furnished - and all of them deserted.

At the broken window, Bollinger leaned out, looked both ways along the snow-swept six-foot-wide setback. They weren't there either.

Reluctantly, he brushed the shards of glass out of his way and crawled through the window.

The storm wind raced over him, pummeled him, stood his hair on end, dashed snowflakes in his face and shoved them down his shirt, under his collar, where they melted on his back. Shivering, he regretted having taken off his overcoat.

Wishing he had handholds of some sort, he stretched out on his belly. The stone was so cold that he felt as if he had lain down bare-chested on a block of ice.

He peered over the edge. Graham Harris was only ten feet below, swinging away from the building on a thin rope, slipping down the line as he followed his arc, swinging back to the building: rappelling.

He reached down, gripped the piton. It was so cold that his fingers almost froze to it. He tried to twist it loose but discovered it was well planted.

Even in the pale, almost nonexistent light, he could see that there was a gate in the snap link that was fixed to the piton. He fingered it, tried to open it, but couldn't figure out how it worked.

Although he was right on top of Harris, Bollinger knew he could not get off an accurate shot. The cold and the wind had brought tears to his eyes, blurring his vision. The light was poor. And the man was moving too fast to make a good target.

Instead, he put down the Walther PPK, rolled onto his side, and quickly extracted a knife from his trousers pocket. He flicked it open. It was the same razor-sharp knife with which he had murdered so many women. And now, if he could cut the rappelling line before Harris got down to the ledge, he would have claimed his first male victim with it. Reaching to the piton, he began to saw through the loop of the knot that was suspended from the jiggling carabiner.

The wind struck the side of the building, rose along the stone, buffeted his face.

He was breathing through his mouth. The air was so cold that it made his throat ache.

Completely unaware of Bollinger, Harris pushed away from the building once more. Swung out, swung back, descended six or eight feet in the process. Pushed out again.

The carabiner was moving on the piton, making it difficult for Bollinger to keep the blade at precisely the same cutting point on the rope.

Harris was rappelling fast, rapidly approaching the ledge where Connie waited for him. In a few seconds he would be safely off the rope.

Finally, after Harris had taken several more steps along the face of the highrise, Bollinger's knife severed the nylon rope; and the line snapped free of the carabiner.

As Graham swooped toward the building, his feet in front of him, intending to take brief possession of a narrow window ledge, he felt the rope go slack.

He knew what had happened.

His thoughts accelerated. Long before the rope had fallen around his shoulders, before his forward momentum was depleted, even as his feet touched the stone, he had considered his situation and decided on a course of action.

The ledge was two inches deep. Just the tips of his boots fitted on it. It wasn't large enough to support him.

Taking advantage of his momentum, he flung himself toward the window and pushed in that direction with his toes - up and in, with all of his strength - the instant he made contact with the window ledge. His shoulder hit one of the tall panes. Glass shattered.

He had hoped to thrust an arm through the glass, then throw it around the center post. If he could do that, he might hold on long enough to open the window and drag himself inside.

However, even as the glass broke, he lost his toehold on the icy two-inch-wide sill. His boots skidded backward, sank through empty air.

He slid down the stonework. He pawed desperately at the window as he went.

His knees struck the sill. The granite tore his trousers, gouged his skin. His knees slipped off the impossibly shallow indention just as his feet had done.

He grabbed the sill with both hands as gravity

drew him over it. He held on as best he could. By his fingers. Dangling over the street. Kicking at the wall with his feet. Trying to find a toehold where there was none. Gasping.

The setback where Connie waited was only fifteen feet from the sill to which he clung, just seven or eight feet from the bottoms of his boots. Eight feet. It looked like a mile to him.

As he contemplated the long fall to Lexington Avenue, he hoped to God that his vision of a bullet in the back had been correct.

His gloves were too thick to serve him well in a precarious position like this. He lost his grip on the ice-sheathed stone.

He dropped onto the yard-wide setback. Landed on his feet. Cried out in pain. Tottered backward.

Connie shouted.

With one foot he stepped into space. Felt death pulling at him. Screamed. Windmilled his arms.

Connie was tethered to the wall and willing to test the piton that she had hammered between the granite blocks. She jumped at Graham, clutched the front of his parka, jerked at him, tried to stagger to safety with him.

For what must have been only a second or two but seemed like an hour, they swayed on the brink.

The wind shoved them toward the street.

But at last she proved sufficiently strong to arrest his backward fall. He brought his foot in from the gulf. They stabilized on the last few inches of stone. Then he threw his arms around her, and they moved back to the face of the building, to safety, away from the concrete canyon.

37

He may have cut the rope,' Connie said, 'but he isn't up there now.'

'He's coming for us.'

'Then he'll cut the rope again.'

'I guess he will. So we'll just have to be too damned fast for him.'

Graham stretched out on the yard-wide ledge, parallel to the side of the building.

His bad leg was filled with a steady almost crippling pain from ankle to hip. Considering all the rappelling he would have to do to reach the street, he was certain the leg would give out at some crucial point in the climb, probably just when his life most depended on surefootedness.

He took a piton from one of the accessory straps at his waist. He held out one hand to Connie. 'Hammer.'

She gave it to him.

He twisted around a bit, lay at an angle to the building, his head and one arm over the edge of the setback.

Far below, an ambulance moved cautiously on Lexington Avenue, its lights flashing. Even from the thirty-third floor, the street was not entirely visible. He could barely make out the lines of the ambulance in the wash of its own emergency beacons. It drew even with the Bowerton Building, then drove on into the snowy night.

He found a mortar seam even without removing his bulky gloves, and he started to pound in a piton.

Suddenly, to one side, two floors below, movement caught his eye. A window opened inward. One of two tall panes. No one appeared at it. However, he sensed the man in the darkness of the office beyond.

A chill passed along his spine; it had nothing to do with the cold or the wind.

Pretending that he had seen nothing, he finished hammering the piton in place. Then he slid away from the edge, stood up. 'We can't go down here,' he told Connie.

She looked puzzled. 'Why not?'

'Bollinger is below us.'

'What?'

'At a window. Waiting to shoot us – or at least you – as we go past him.'

Her gray eyes were wide. 'But why didn't he come here to get us?'

'Maybe he thought we'd already started down. Or maybe he thought we'd run out of his reach along this setback the moment he came into an office on this floor.'

'What now?'

'I'm thinking.'

'I'm scared.'

'Don't be.'

'Can't help it.'

Her eyebrows were crusted with snow, as was the fringe of fur lining that escaped her hood. He held her. The wind moaned incessantly.

He said, 'This is a corner building.'

'Does that matter?'

'It faces on another street besides Lexington.'

'So?'

'So we follow the setback,' he said excitedly. 'Turn the corner on the setback.'

'And climb down the other face, the one that overlooks the side street?'

'You've got it. That's no harder to climb than this wall.'

'And Bollinger can only see Lexington Avenue from his window,' she said.

'That's right.'

'Brilliant.'

'Let's do it.'

'Sooner or later, he'll figure out what we've done.'

'Later.'

'It had better be.'

'Sure. He'll wait right where he is for a few minutes, expecting to pick us off. Then he'll waste time checking this entire floor.'

'And the stairwells.'

'And the elevator shafts. We might get most of the way down before he finds us.'

'Okay,' she said. She unhooked her safety tether from the window post.

38

At the open window on the thirty-first floor, Frank Bollinger waited. Apparently they were preparing the rope which they would hook to the piton that Harris had just pounded into place.

He looked forward to shooting the woman as she came past him on the line. The image excited him. He would enjoy blowing her away into the night.

When that happened, Harris would be stunned, emotionally destroyed, unable to think fast, unable to protect himself. Then Bollinger could go after him at will. If he could kill Harris where he chose, kill him cleanly, he could salvage the plan that he and Billy had devised this afternoon.

As he waited for his prey, he thought again of that second night of his relationship with Billy. . . .

After the whore left Billy's apartment, they ate dinner in the kitchen. Between them they consumed two salads, four steaks, four rashers of bacon, six eggs, eight pieces of toast, and a large quantity of Scotch. They approached the food as they had the woman: with intensity, with single-mindedness, with appetites that were not those of men but those of supermen.

At midnight, over brandy, Bollinger had talked

about the years when he had lived with his grandmother.

Even now he could remember any part of that conversation he wished. He was blessed with virtually total recall, a talent honed by years of memorizing complex poetry.

'So she called you Dwight. I like that name.'

'Why are you talking that way?'

'The Southern accent? I was born in the South. I had an accent until I was twenty. I made a concerted effort to lose it. Took voice lessons. But I can recall it when I want. Sometimes the drawl amuses me.'

'Why did you take voice lessons in the first place? The accent is nice.'

'Nobody up North takes you seriously when you've got a heavy drawl. They think you're a redneck. Say, what if I call you Dwight?'

'If you want.'

'I'm closer to you than anyone's been since your grandmother. Isn't that true?'

'Yeah.'

'I should call you Dwight. In fact, I'm closer to you than your grandmother was.'

'I guess so.'

'And you know me better than anyone else does.'

'Do I? I suppose I do.'

'Then we need special names for each other.'

'So call me Dwight. I like it.'

'And you call me – Billy.'

'Billy?'

'Billy James Plover.'

'Where'd you get that?'

'I was born with it.'

'You changed your name?'

'Just like I did the accent.'

'When?'

'A long time ago.'

'Why?'

'I went to college up North. Didn't do as well as I should have done. Didn't get the grades I deserved. Finally dropped out. But by then I knew why I didn't make it. In those days, Ivy League professors didn't give you a chance if you spoke with a drawl and had a redneck name like Billy James Plover.'

'You're exaggerating.'

'How would you know? How in the hell would you know? You've always had a nice white Anglo-Saxon Protestant Northern name. Franklin Dwight Bollinger. What would you know about it?'

'I guess you're right.'

'At that time, all the Ivy League intellectuals were involved in a conspiracy of sorts against the South, against Southerners. They still are, except that the conspiracy isn't so broad or so vicious as it once was. Back then, the only way you could succeed in a Northern university or community was to have an Anglo-Saxon name like yours – or else one that was out-and-out Jewish. Frank Bollinger or Sol Cohen. You could be accepted with either name. But not with Billy James Plover.'

'So you stopped being Billy.'

'As soon as I could.'

'And did your luck improve?'

'The same day I changed my name.'

'But you want me to call you Billy.'

'It wasn't the name that was wrong. It was the people who reacted negatively to the name.'

'Billy . . .'

'Shouldn't we have special names for each other?'

'Doesn't matter. If you want.'

'Aren't we special ourselves, Frank?'

'I think so.'

'Aren't we different from other people?'

'Quite different.'

'So we shouldn't use between us the names they call us by.'

'If you say so.'

'We're supermen, Frank.'

'What?'

'Not like Clark Kent.'

'I sure don't have X-ray vision.'

'Supermen as Nietzsche meant.'

'Nietzsche?'

'You aren't familiar with his work?'

'Not particularly.'

'I'll lend you a book by him.'

'Okay.'

'In fact, since Nietzsche should be read over and over again. I'll give you a book by him.'

'Thank you . . . Billy.'

'You're welcome, Dwight.'

At the half-open window, Bollinger glanced at his watch. The time was 12:30.

Neither Harris nor the woman had started down from the thirty-third-floor setback.

He couldn't wait any longer. He had squandered too much time already. He would have to go looking for them.

39

Connie hammered a piton into a horizontal mortar seam. She hooked the safety tether to the piton with a carabiner, then untied herself from the main line.

The moment it was free, Graham reeled up the rope.

Climbing this face of the building was proving easier than scaling the front on Lexington Avenue. Not that there was a greater number of setbacks, ledges or foot-holds here than there; the distribution of those was the same. However, the wind was much less fierce on the side street than it had been on Lexington. Here, the snowflakes that struck her face *felt* like snowflakes and not like tiny bullets. The cold air hugged her legs, but it did not press *through* her jeans; it didn't pinch her thighs and stab painfully into her calves as it had done earlier.

She had descended ten floors - and Graham five - since they had seen Bollinger waiting for them at the window. Graham had lowered her to the yard-wide twenty-eighth-floor setback and had rappelled down after her. Below that point there was only one other setback, this one at the sixth floor, three hundred and thirty feet down. At the twenty-third level, there was an eighteen-inch-wide decorative ledge – quintessential art deco; the stone was carved into a band of connected, abstract bunches of grapes – and they made that their next goal. Graham belayed her, and she found that the carved ledge was large and strong enough to support her. In less than a minute, powered by his new-found confidence, he would be beside her.

She had no idea what they would do after that. The sixth-floor setback was still a long way off; figuring five yards to a floor, that haven lay two hundred and fifty-five feet below. Their ropes were only one hundred feet long. Between this ledge of stone grapes and the sixth story, there was nothing but a sheer wall and impossibly narrow window ledges.

Graham had assured her that they were not at a dead end. Nevertheless, she was worried.

Overhead, he began to rappel through the falling snow. She was fascinated by the sight. He seemed to be creating the line as he went, weaving it out of his own substance; he resembled a spider that was swinging gracefully, smoothly on its own silk from one point to another on a web that it was constructing.

In seconds he was standing beside her.

She gave him the hammer.

He placed two pitons in the wall between the windows, in different horizontal mortar seams.

He was breathing hard; mist plumed from his open mouth.

'You all right?' she asked.

'So far.'

Without benefit of a safety line, he sidled along the ledge, away from her, his back to the street, his hands pressed against the stone. On this side of the building, the gentler wind had formed miniature drifts on the ledges and on the windowsills. He was putting his feet down in two or three inches of snow and, here and there, on patches of brittle ice.

Connie wanted to ask him where he was going, what he was doing; but she was afraid that if she talked she would distract him and he would fall.

Past the window, he stopped and pounded in another piton, then hung the hammer on the accessory strap at his waist.

He returned, inch by inch to where he had placed the first two pegs. He snapped his safety harness to one of those pitons.

'What was all that for?' she asked.

'We're going to rappel down a few floors,' he said. 'Both of us. At the same time. On two separate ropes.'

Swallowing hard, she said, 'Not me.'

'Yes, you.'

Her heart was thumping so furiously that she thought it might burst. 'I can't do it.'

'You can. You will.'

She shook her head: no.

'You won't rappel the way I've done.'

'That's for damned sure.'

'I've been doing a body rappel. You'll go down in a seat rappel. It's safer and easier.'

Although none of her doubts had been allayed, Connie said, 'What's the difference between a body rappel and a seat rappel?'

'I'll show you in a minute.'

'Take your time.'

He grabbed the hundred-foot line on which he had descended from the twenty-eight-floor setback. He tugged on it three times, jerked it to the right.

Five stories above them, the knot came loose; the rope snaked down.

He caught the line, piled it beside him.

He examined the end of it to see if it was worn, and was satisfied that it wasn't. He tied a knot in it, looped the rope through the gate of the carabiner. He snapped the carabiner to the free piton that was one mortar seam above the peg that anchored his safety tether.

'We can't rappel all the way to the street,' Connie said.

'Sure we can.'

'The ropes aren't long enough.'

'You'll rappel just five floors at a time. Brace yourself on a window ledge. Then let go of the rappelling line with your right hand –'

'Brace myself on a two-inch sill?'

'It can be done. Don't forget, you'll still be holding onto the line with your left hand.'

'Meanwhile, what will my right hand be doing?'

'Smashing in both panes of the window.'

'And then?'

'First, attach your safety tether to the window. Second, snap another carabiner to the center post. As soon as that's done, you take your weight off the main line and then –'

'Tug on it,' Connie said, 'pull apart the overhead knot like you did just a minute ago.'

'I'll show you how.'

'I catch the line as it falls?'

'Yes.'

'And tie it to the carabiner that I've linked to the window post.'

'That's right.'

Her legs were cold. She stamped her feet on the

ledge. 'I guess then I unhook my safety line and rappel down five more floors.'

'And brace yourself in another window and repeat the entire routine. We'll go all the way to the street, but only five stories at a time.'

'You make it sound simple.'

'You'll manage better than you think. I'll show you how to use a seat rappel.'

'There's another problem.'

'What?'

'I don't know how to tie one of those knots that can be jerked loose from below.'

'It isn't difficult. I'll show you.'

He untied the main line from the carabiner in front of him.

She leaned close to him and bent over the rope that he held in both hands. The world-famous glow of Manhattan's millions of bright lights was screened by the storm. Below, the rimed pavement of the street reflected the light from the many street lamps; but that illumination scarcely affected the purple shadows twenty-three floors above. Nevertheless, if she squinted, she could see what Graham was doing.

In a few minutes, she learned how to attach the rope to the anchor point so that it could be retrieved. She tied it several times to make sure she would not forget how it was done.

Next, Graham looped a sling around her hips and through her crotch. He joined the three end-points of the rope with yet another carabiner.

'Now, about this rappelling,' she said as she gripped the main line. She manufactured a smile that he probably did not see, and she tried not to sound terrified.

Taking another snap link from the accessory strap at his waist, Graham said, 'First, I've got to link the main line to the sling. Then I'll show you how you should stand to begin the rappel. I'll explain –'

He was interrupted by the muffled report of a gun: *whump!*

Connie looked up.

Bollinger wasn't above them.

She wondered if she actually had heard a gun or whether the noise might have been produced by the wind.

Then she heard it again: *whump!* There was no doubt. A shot. Two shots. Very close. Inside the building. Somewhere on the twenty-third floor.

Frank Bollinger pushed open the broken door, went into the office, switched on the lights. He stepped around the receptionist's desk, around a typewriter stand and a Xerox copier. He hurried toward the windows that overlooked the side street.

When the lights came on behind the windows on both sides of them, Graham unhooked his safety tether from the piton and told Connie to unhook her own five-foot line.

There was a noise at the window on their right as Bollinger pushed up the rusty latch.

'Follow me,' Graham said.

He was perspiring again. His face was slick with sweat. Under the hood, his moist scalp itched.

He turned away from Connie, from the window that Bollinger was about to open, turned to his left, toward Lexington Avenue. Without benefit of a safety line, he walked the narrow ledge instead of sidling along it. He kept his right hand on the granite for what little sense of security it gave him. He had to place each foot directly in front of the other, as if he were on a tightrope, for the ledge was not wide enough to allow him to walk naturally.

He was fifty feet from the Lexington Avenue face of the highrise. When he and Connie turned the corner on the ledge, they would be out of the line of fire.

Of course, Bollinger would find an office with windows that had a view of Lexington. At most they would gain only a minute or two. But right now, an extra minute of life was worth any effort.

He wanted to look back to see if Connie was having any difficulty, but he didn't dare. He had to keep his eyes on the ledge ahead of him and carefully judge the placement of each boot.

Before he had gone more than ten feet, he heard Bollinger shouting.

He hunched his shoulders, remembering the psychic vision, anticipating the bullet.

With a shock he realized that Connie was shielding him. He should have sent her ahead, should have placed himself between her and the pistol. If she stopped a bullet that was meant for him, he didn't want to live. However, it was much too late for him to relinquish the lead. If they stopped they would make even better targets than they already were.

A shot cracked in the darkness.

Then another.

He began to walk faster than was prudent, aware that a misstep would plummet him to the street. His feet slipped on the snow-sheathed stone.

The corner was thirty feet away.

Twenty-five . . .

Bollinger fired again.

Twenty feet.

He felt the fourth shot before he heard it. The bullet ripped open the left sleeve of his parka, seared through the upper part of his arm.

The impact of the slug made him stumble a bit. He lumbered forward a few quick, unplanned steps. The street appeared to spin wildly below him. With his right hand he pawed helplessly at the side of the building. He put one foot down on the edge of the stone, his heel in empty air. He heard himself shouting but hardly knew what he was saying. His boots gripped in the drifted snow, but they skidded on a patch of ice. When he regained his balance within half a dozen steps, he was amazed that he hadn't fallen.

At first there was no pain in his arm. He was numb from the shoulder down. It was as if his arm had been blown off. For an instant he wondered if he had been mortally wounded; but he realized that a direct hit would have had more force, would have knocked him off his feet and pitched him off the ledge. In a minute or two the wound would begin to hurt like hell, but it wouldn't kill him.

Fifteen feet . . .

He was dizzy.

His legs felt weak.

Probably shock, he thought.

Ten feet.

Another shot. Not so loud as the ones that had come before it. Not as frighteningly close. Fifteen yards away.

At the corner, as he started to inch around onto the Lexington Avenue face of the highrise where a violent wind wrenched at him, he was able to glance back the way he had come. Behind him, the ledge was empty.

Connie was gone.

40

Connie was four or five yards below the twenty-third-floor ledge of stone grapes, swinging slightly, suspended over the street. She couldn't bear to look down.

Arms extended above her, she held the nylon rope with both hands. She had considerable difficulty maintaining her grip. Strain had numbed her fingers, and she could no longer be certain that she was clutching the line tightly enough to save herself. A moment ago, relaxing her hands without realizing what she was doing, she had slipped down the rope as if it were well greased, covering two yards in a split second before she was able to halt herself.

She had tried to find toeholds. There were none.

She fixed her gaze on the ledge overhead. She expected to see Bollinger.

Minutes ago, when he opened the window on her right and leaned out with the pistol in one hand, she had known at once that he was too close to miss her. She couldn't follow Graham toward the Lexington Avenue corner. If she tried that, she would be shot in the back. Instead, she gripped the main line and tried to anticipate the shot. If she had even the slimmest chance of escaping – and she was not convinced that she had – then she would have to act only a fraction of a second *before* the explosion came. If she didn't move until or after he fired, she might be dead, and she would certainly be too late to fool him. Fortunately, her timing was perfect; she jumped backward into the void just as he fired, so he must have thought he hit her.

She prayed he would think she was dead. If he had any doubt, he would crawl part of the way through the window, lean over the ledge, see her – and cut the rope.

Although her own plight was serious enough to require all of her attention, she was worried about Graham. She knew that he hadn't been shot off the ledge, for she would have seen him as he fell past her. He was still up there, but he might be badly wounded.

Whether or not he was hurt, her life depended on his coming back to look for her.

She was not a climber. She didn't know how to rappel. She didn't know how to secure her position on the rope. She didn't know how to do anything but hang there; and she wouldn't be able to do even that much longer.

She didn't want to die, *refused* to die. Even if Graham had been killed already, she didn't want to follow him into death. She loved him more than she had ever loved anyone else. At times she became frustrated because she could not find the words to express the breadth and depth of her feeling for him. The language of love was inadequate. She ached for him. But she cherished life as well. Getting up in the morning and making French toast for breakfast. Working in the antique shop. Reading a good book. Going out to an exciting movie. So many small delights. Perhaps it was true that the little joys of daily life were insignificant when compared to the intense pleasures of love, but if she was to be denied the ultimate, she would settle willingly for second best. She knew that her attitude in no way cheapened her love for Graham or made suspect the bonds between them. Her love of life was what had drawn him to her and made her so right for him. To Connie, there was but one obscenity, and that was the grave.

Fifteen feet above, someone moved in the light that radiated through the open window.

Bollinger?

Oh, Jesus, no!

But before she could give in to despair, Graham's face came out of the shadows. He saw her and was stunned. Obviously, he had expected her to be twenty-three stories below, a crumpled corpse on the snow-covered pavement.

'Help me,' she said.

Grinning, he began to reel her up.

In the twenty-third-floor corridor, Frank Bollinger stopped to reload his pistol. He was nearly out of ammunition.

'So you read Nietzsche last night. What did you think?'

'I agree with him.'

'About what?'

'Everything.'

'Supermen?'

'Especially that.'

'Why especially?'

'He has to be right. Mankind as we know it has to be an intermediate stage in evolution. Otherwise, everything is so pointless.'

'Aren't we the kind of men he was talking about?'

'It sure as hell seems to me that we are. But one thing bothers me. I've always thought of myself as a liberal. In politics.'

'So?'

'How do I reconcile liberal, left-of-center politics with a belief in a superior race?'

'No problem, Dwight. Pure, hard-core liberals believe in a superior race. They think they're it. They believe they're more intelligent than the general run of mankind, better suited than the little people are to manage the little people's lives. They think they have the one true vision, the ability to solve all the moral dilemmas of the century. They prefer big government because that is the first step to totalitarianism, toward unquestioned rule by the elite. And of course they see themselves as the elite. Reconcile Nietzsche with liberal politics? That's no more difficult than reconciling it with extreme right-wing philosophy.'

Bollinger stopped in front of the door to Opway Electronics, because that office had windows that overlooked Lexington Avenue. He fired the Walther PPK twice; the lock disintegrated under the bullets' impact.

Suggesting ways that she could help herself, favoring his injured left arm, Graham pulled Connie onto the ledge.

Weeping, he hugged her with both arms, squeezed her so tightly that he would have cut off her breath if they hadn't been wearing the goose-down parkas. They swayed on the narrow ledge; and for the moment they were unaware of the long drop beside them, temporarily unimpressed by the danger. He didn't want to let go of her, not ever. He felt as if he had taken a drug, an upper, something to boost his spirits. Considering their circumstances, his mood was unrealistic. Although they were a long way, both in time and in distance, from safety, he was elated; she was alive.

'Where's Bollinger?' she asked.

Behind Graham, the office was full of light, the window open. But there was no sign of the killer.

'He probably went to look for me on the Lexington side,' Graham said.

'Then he *does* think I'm dead.'

'He must. *I* thought you were.'

'What's happened to your arm?'

'He shot me.'

'Oh, no!'

'It hurts. And it feels stiff, but that's all.'

'There's a lot of blood.'

'Not much. The bullet probably cauterized the wound; that's how shallow it is.' He held out his left hand, opened and closed it to show her that he wasn't seriously affected. 'I can climb.'

'You shouldn't.'

'I'll be fine. Besides, I don't have a choice.'

'We could go inside, use the stairs again.'

'As soon as Bollinger checks the Lexington side and doesn't find me, he'll come back. If I'm not here, he'll look on the stairs. He'd nail us if we tried to go that way.'

'Now what?'

'Same as before. We'll walk this ledge to the corner. By the time we get to Lexington, he'll have looked over that face of the building and be gone. Then we'll rappel.'

'With your arm like this?'

'With my arm like this.'

'The vision you had about being shot in the back –'

'What about it?'

She touched his left arm. 'Was this it?'

'No.'

Bollinger turned away from the window that opened onto Lexington Avenue. He hurried out of the Opway Electronics suite and down the hall toward the office from which he had shot at Harris a few minutes ago.

'Chaos, Dwight.'

'Chaos?'

'There are too damned many of these subhumans for the supermen to take control of things in ordinary times. Only in the midst of Armageddon will men like us ascend.'

'You mean . . . after a nuclear war?'

'That's one way it could happen. Only men like us would have the courage and imagination to lead civilization out of the ruins. But wouldn't it be ridiculous to wait until they've destroyed everything we should inherit?'

'Ridiculous.'

'So it's occurred to me that we could generate the chaos we need, bring about Armageddon in a less destructive form.'

'How?'

'Well. . . does the name Albert DeSalvo mean anything to you?'

'No.'

'He was the Boston Strangler.'

'Oh, yeah. He murdered a lot of women.'

'We should study DeSalvo's case. He wasn't one of us, of course. He was an inferior and a psychotic to boot. But I think we should use him as a model. Single-handedly, he created so much fear that he almost threw the city of Boston into a state of panic. Fear would be our basic tool. Fear can be stoked into panic. A handful of panic-stricken people can transmit their hysteria to the entire population of a city or country.'

'But DeSalvo didn't come close to creating the kind of – or the degree of – chaos that would lead to the collapse of society.'

'Because that wasn't his goal.'

'Even if it had been –'

'Dwight, suppose an Albert DeSalvo . . . better yet, suppose a Jack the Ripper were loose in Manhattan. Suppose he murdered not just ten women, not twenty, but a hundred. Two hundred. In a particularly brutal fashion. With clear evidence of aberrant sex in every case. So there was no doubt that they all died by the same hand. And what if he did all of this in a few months?'

'There would be fear. But –'

'It would be the biggest news story in the city, in the state, and probably in the country. Then suppose that after we murdered the first hundred women, we began to spend half our time killing men. Each time, we'd cut off the man's sex organ and leave behind a message attributing the murder to a fictitious militant feminist group.

'What?'

'We'd make the public think the men were being murdered in retaliation for the murders of the hundred women.'

'Except women don't typically commit crimes like that.'

'Doesn't matter. We're not trying to create a typical situation.'

'I'm not sure I understand what sort of situation we are trying to create.'

'Don't you see? There are damned ugly tensions between men and women in this country. Hideous tensions. Year by year, as the women's liberation movement has grown, those tensions have become almost unbearable, because they're repressed, hidden. We'll make them boil to the surface.'

'It's not bad. You're exaggerating.'

'I'm not. Believe me. I know. And don't you see what else? There are hundreds of potential psychotic killers out there. All they need is to be given some direction, a little push. They'll hear about and read about the killings so much that they'll get ideas of their own. Once we've cut up a hundred women and twenty or so men, pretending to be psychotic ourselves, we'll have a dozen imitators doing our work for us.'

'Maybe.'

'Definitely. All mass murderers have had their imitators. But none of them has ever committed crimes grand enough to inspire legions of mimics. We will. And then when we've turned out a squad of sex killers, we'll shift the direction of our own activities.'

'Shift to what?'

'We'll murder white people at random and use a fictitious black revolutionary group to claim credit. After a dozen killings of that sort –'

'We could knock off some blacks and leave every-

one under the impression they were killed in retaliation.'

'You've got it. Fan the flames.'

'I'm beginning to see your point. In a city this size, there are countless factions. Blacks, whites, Puerto Ricans, Orientals, men, women, liberals, conservatives, radicals and reactionaries, Catholics and Jews, rich and poor, young and old. . . . We could try to turn each against its opposite and all of them against one another. Once factional violence begins, whether it's religious or political or economic, it usually escalates endlessly.'

'Exactly. If we planned carefully enough, we could do it. In six months, you'd have at least two thousand dead. Maybe five times that number.'

'And you'd have martial law. That would put an end to it before there was chaos on the scale you've talked about.'

'We might have martial law. But we'd still have chaos. In Northern Ireland they've had soldiers on street corners for years, but the killing goes on. Oh, there'd be chaos, Dwight. And it would spread to other cities as –'

'No. I can't swallow that.'

'All over the country, people would be reading and hearing about New York. They'd –'

'It wouldn't spread that easily, Billy.'

'All right. All right. But there would be chaos here, at least. The voters would be ready to elect a tough-talking mayor with new ideas.'

'Certainly.'

'We could elect one of us, one of the new race. The mayoralty of New York is a good political base for a smart man who wants the presidency.'

'The voters might elect a political strongman. But

not every political strongman is going to be one of our people.'

'If we planned the chaos, we could also plan to run one of our men in the wake of it. He would know what was coming; he'd have an inside track.'

'One of our men? Hell, we don't know any but you and me.'

'I'd make an excellent mayor.'

'You?'

'I have a good base for a campaign.'

'Christ, come to think of it, you do.'

'I could win.'

'You'd have a fair chance, anyway.'

'It would be a step up the ladder of power for our kind, our race.'

'Jesus, the killing we'd have to do!'

'Haven't you ever killed?'

'A pimp. Two drug pushers who pulled guns on me. A whore that nobody knows about.'

'Did killing disturb you?'

'No. They were scum.'

'We'd be killing scum. Our inferiors. Animals.'

'Could we get away with it?'

'We both know cops. What would cops look for? Known mental patients. Known criminals. Known radicals. People with some sort of motive. We have a motive, but they'd never figure it in a million years.'

'If we worked out every detail, planned carefully – hell, we might do it.'

'Do you know what Leopold wrote to Loeb before they murdered Bobby Franks? "The superman is not liable for anything he may do, except for the one crime that it is possible for him to commit – to make a mistake."'

'If we did something like this –'

'If?'

'You're committed to it?'

'Aren't you, Dwight?'

'We'd start with women?'

'Yes.'

'Kill them'

'Yes.'

'Billy . . .?'

'Yes?'

'Rape them first?'

'Oh, yes.'

'It could even be fun.'

Bollinger leaned out of the window, looked both ways along the ledge. Harris was not on the face of the building that overlooked the side street.

Although the pitons were wedged in the stone beside the window, as they had been when he'd fired at Harris, the rope that had been attached to one of them was gone.

Bollinger crawled onto the windowsill, leaned out much too far, peered over the ledge. The woman's body should have been on the street below. But there was no corpse. Nothing but the smooth sheen of fresh snow.

Dammit, she hadn't fallen! He hadn't shot the bitch after all!

Why wouldn't these people *die?*

Furious, he stumbled back into the room, out of the wind-whipped snow. He left the office and followed the corridor to the nearest stairwell.

Connie wished that she could rappel with her eyes closed. Balanced on the side of the highrise, twenty-three stories above Lexington Avenue, without a safety tether, she was unnerved by the scene.

Right hand behind.

Left hand in front.

Right hand to brake.

Left hand to guide.

Feet spread and planted firmly on the wall.

Repeating to herself all that Graham had taught her, she pushed away from the building. And gasped. She felt as if she had taken a suicidal leap.

As she swung out, she realized that she was clenching the rope too tightly with her left hand. Left to guide. *Right* to brake. She relaxed her grip on the rope in front of her and slid down a few feet before braking.

She approached the building improperly. Her legs were not straight out in front of her, and they weren't rigid enough. They buckled. She twisted to the right, out of control, and struck the granite with her shoulder. The impact was not great enough to break a bone, but it was much too hard.

It dazed her, but she didn't let go of the rope. Got her feet against the stone once more. Got into position. Shook her head to clear it. Glanced to her left. Saw Graham three yards away on that side. Nodded so he would know that she was all right. Then pushed outward. Pushed hard. Slid down. Swung back. She didn't make any mistakes this time.

Grinning, Graham watched as Connie took a few more steps down the stone. Her endurance and determination delighted him. There really was some Nora Charles in her. And a hell of a lot of Nick too.

When he saw that she had pretty much gotten the knack of rappelling – her style was crude but adequate – he kicked away from the wall. He descended farther than she did on each arc and reached the eighteenth floor ahead of her.

He braced himself on the almost nonexistent window ledge. He smashed in the two tall panes of glass and fixed a snap link to the metal center post. When he had attached his safety tether to that carabiner, he released the main line, pulled it free of the overhead anchor. He caught the rope, tied it to the carabiner in front of him, and took up a rappelling position.

Beside him, nine feet away, Connie was also ready to rappel.

He flung himself into space.

He was amazed not only at how well he remembered the skills and techniques of a climber, but at how quickly the worst of his fear had vanished. He was still afraid, but not unnaturally so. Necessity and Connie's love had produced a miracle that no psychiatrist could have matched.

He was beginning to think they might escape. His left arm ached where the bullet had grazed it, and the fingers of that hand were stiff. The pain in his bad leg had subsided to a continuous dull throb that made him grit his teeth occasionally but which didn't interfere too much with his rappelling.

In a couple of steps he reached the seventeenth floor. In two more jumps he came to rest against the sixteenth-story window ledge – where Frank Bollinger had decided to set up an ambush.

The window was closed. However, the drapes had been drawn back. One desk lamp glowed dimly in the office.

Bollinger was on the other side of the glass, a huge silhouette. He was just lifting the latch.

No! Graham thought.

In the same instant that his boots touched the window ledge, he kicked away from it.

Bollinger saw him and pulled off a shot without bothering to open the rectangular panes. Glass sliced into the night.

Although Bollinger reacted fast, Graham was already out of his line of fire. He swung back to the wall seven or eight feet below Bollinger, rappelled again, stopped at the fifteenth-story window.

He looked up and saw flame flicker briefly from the muzzle of the pistol as Bollinger shot at Connie.

The gunfire threw her off her pace. She hit the wall with her shoulder again. Frantic, she got her feet under her and rappelled.

Bollinger fired again.

41

Bollinger knew that he hadn't scored a hit on either of them.

He left the office, ran to the elevator. He switched on the control panel and pushed the button for the tenth floor.

As the lift descended, he thought about the plan that he and Billy had formulated yesterday.

'You'll kill Harris first. Do what you want with the woman, but be sure to cut her up.'

'I always cut them up. That was my idea in the first place.'

'You should kill Harris where it'll cause the least mess, where you can clean up after.'

'Clean up?'

'When you're done with the woman, you'll go back to Harris, wipe up every speck of blood around him, and wrap his body in a plastic tarp. So don't kill him on a carpet where he'll leave stains. Take him into a room with a tile floor. Maybe a bathroom.'

'Wrap him in a tarp?'

'I'll be waiting behind the Bowerton Building at ten o'clock. You'll bring the body to me. We'll put it in the car. Later, we can take it out of the city, bury it upstate someplace.'

'Bury it? Why?'

'We're going to try to make the police think that Harris has killed his own fiancée, that he's the Butcher. I'll disguise my voice and call Homicide. I'll claim to be Harris, and I'll tell them I'm the Butcher.'

'To mislead them?'

'You've got it.'

'Sooner or later they'll smell a trick.'

'Yes, they will. Eventually. But for a few weeks, maybe even for a few months, they'll be after Harris. There wouldn't be any chance whatsoever that they'd follow a good lead, one that might bring them to us.'

'A classic red herring.'

'Precisely.'

'It'll give us time.'

'Yes.'

'To do everything we want.'

'Nearly everything.'

The plan was ruined.

The clairvoyant was too damned hard to kill.

The doors of the lift slid apart.

Bollinger tripped coming out of the elevator. He fell. The pistol flew out of his hand, clattered against the wall.

He got to his knees and wiped the sweat out of his eyes.

He said, 'Billy?'

But he was alone.

Coughing, sniffling, he crawled to the pistol, clutched it in his right hand and stood up.

He went into the dark hall, to the door of an office that would have a view of Lexington.

Because he was worried about running out of ammunition, he used only one shot on the door. He aimed carefully. The *boom!* echoed and reechoed in the corridor. The lock was damaged, but it wouldn't release altogether. The door rattled in its frame. Rather than use another bullet, he put his shoulder to the panel, pressed until it gave inward.

By the time he reached the Lexington Avenue windows, Harris and the woman had passed him. They were two floors below.

He returned to the elevator. He was going to have to go outside and confront them when they reached the street. He pushed the button for the ground floor.

Braced against the [illegible] agreed to cover the [illegible] in two equal [illegible] dow posts as their [illegible]

At the fourth [illegible] rectangular panes, [illegible] post, hooked his [illegible] jerked [illegible] foot to the right of the [illegible]

He [illegible] slightly and looked [illegible]

Bollinger, [illegible] stood on the snow [illegible] below.

[illegible] Get inside! Through the [illegible]

Bollinger fired [illegible]

A burst of [illegible] back.

Is this where [illegible]

Desperately, [illegible] punch out the shards of glass that [illegible] window frame. [illegible] was about to drag himself inside [illegible]

42

Braced against the eighth-floor windows, they agreed to cover the final hundred and twenty feet in two equal rappels, using the fourth-floor window posts as their last anchor points.

At the fourth level, Graham smashed in both rectangular panes. He snapped a carabiner to the post, hooked his safety tether to the carabiner, and jerked involuntarily as a bullet slapped the stone a foot to the right of his head.

He knew at once what had happened. He turned slightly and looked down.

Bollinger, in shirt sleeves and looking harried, stood on the snow-shrouded sidewalk, sixty feet below.

Motioning to Connie, Graham shouted, 'Go in! Get inside! Through the window!'

Bollinger fired again.

A burst of light, pain, blood: a bullet in the back . . .

Is this where it happens? he wondered.

Desperately, Graham used his gloved fist to punch out the shards of glass that remained in the window frame. He grabbed the center post and was about to drag himself inside when the street behind him was suddenly filled with a curious rumbling.

A big yellow road grader turned the corner into Lexington Avenue. Its large black tires churned through the slush and spewed out an icy liquid behind. The plow on the front of the machine was six feet high and ten feet across. Emergency beacons flashed on the roof of the operator's cab. Two headlights the size of dinner plates popped up like the eyes of a frog, glared through the falling snow.

It was the only vehicle in sight on the storm-clogged street.

Graham glanced at Connie. She seemed to be having trouble disentangling herself from the lines and getting through the window. He turned away from her, waved urgently at the driver of the grader. The man could barely be seen behind the dirty windshield. 'Help!' Graham shouted. He didn't think the man could hear him over the roar of the engine. Nevertheless, he kept shouting. 'Help! Up here! Help us!'

Connie began to shout too.

Surprised, Bollinger did exactly what he should not have done. He whirled and shot at the grader.

The driver braked, almost came to a full stop.

'Help!' Graham shouted.

Bollinger fired at the machine again. The slug ricocheted off the steel that framed the windshield of the cab.

The driver shifted gears and gunned the engine.

Bollinger ran.

Lifted by hydraulic arms, the plow rose a foot off the pavement. It cleared the curb as the machine lumbered onto the sidewalk.

Pursued by the grader, Bollinger ran thirty or

forty feet along the walk before he sprinted into the street. Kicking up small clouds of snow with each step, he crossed the avenue, with the plow close behind him.

Connie was rapt.

Bollinger let the grader close the distance between them. When only two yards separated him from the shining steel blade, he dashed to one side, out of its way. He ran past the machine, came back toward the Bowerton Building.

The grader didn't turn as easily as a sports car. By the time the driver had brought it around and was headed back, Bollinger was standing under Graham again.

Graham saw him raise the gun. It glinted in the light from the street lamp.

At ground level where the wind was a bit less fierce, the shot was very loud. The bullet cracked into the granite by Graham's right foot.

The grader bore down on Bollinger, horn blaring.

He put his back to the building and faced the mechanical behemoth.

Sensing what the madman would do, Graham fumbled with the compact, battery-powered rock drill that was clipped to his waist belt. He got it free of the strap.

The grader was fifteen to twenty feet from Bollinger, who aimed the pistol at the windshield of the operator's cab.

From his perch on the fourth floor, Graham threw the rock drill. It arced through sixty feet of falling snow and hit Bollinger – not a solid blow on the head, as Graham had hoped, but on the hip. It glanced off him with little force.

Nevertheless, the drill startled Bollinger. He jumped, put a foot on ice, pitched forward, stumbled off the curb, skidded with peculiar grace in the snow, and sprawled face-down in the gutter.

The driver of the grader had expected his quarry to run away; instead, Bollinger fell toward the machine, into it. The operator braked, but he could not bring the grader to a full stop within only eight feet.

The huge steel plow was raised twelve inches off the street; but that was not quite high enough to pass safely over Bollinger. The bottom of the blade caught him at the buttocks and gouged through his flesh, rammed his head, crushed his skull, jammed his body against the raised curb.

Blood sprayed across the snow in the circle of light beneath the nearest street lamp.

43

MacDonald, Ott, the security guards and the building engineer had been tucked into heavy plastic body bags supplied by the city morgue. The bags were lined up on the marble floor.

Near the shuttered newsstand at the front of the lobby, half a dozen folding chairs had been arranged in a semicircle. Graham and Connie sat there with Ira Preduski and three other policemen.

Preduski was in his usual condition: slightly bedraggled. His brown suit hung on him only marginally better than a sheet would have done. Because he had been walking in the snow, his trouser cuffs were damp. His shoes and socks were wet. He wasn't wearing galoshes or boots; he owned a pair of the former and two pairs of the latter, but he never remembered to put them on in bad weather.

'Now, I don't mean to mother you,' Preduski said to Graham. 'I know I've asked before. And you've told me. But I'm worried. I can't help it. I worry unnecessarily about a lot of things. That's another fault of mine. But what about your arm? Where you were shot. Is it all right?'

Graham lightly patted the bandage under his

shirt. A paramedic with bad breath but sure hands had attended to him an hour ago. 'I'm just fine.'

'What about your leg?'

Graham grimaced. 'I'm no more crippled now than I was before all this happened.'

Turning to Connie, Preduski said, 'What about you? The doc with the ambulance says you've got some bad bruises.'

'Just bruises,' she said almost airily. She was holding Graham's hand. 'Nothing worse.'

'Well, you've both had a terrible night. Just awful. And it's my fault. I should have caught Bollinger weeks ago. If I'd had half a brain, I'd have wrapped up this case long before you two got involved.' He looked at his watch. 'Almost three in the morning.' He stood up, tried unsuccessfully to straighten the rumpled collar of his overcoat. 'We've kept you here much too long. Much too long. But I'm going to have to ask you to hang around fifteen or twenty minutes more to answer any questions that the other detectives or forensics men might have. Is that too much to ask? Would you mind? I know it's a terrible, terrible imposition. I apologize.'

'It's all right,' Graham said wearily.

Preduski spoke to another plainclothes detective sitting with the group. 'Jerry, will you be sure they aren't kept more than fifteen or twenty minutes?'

'Whatever you say, Ira.' Jerry was a tall, chunky man in his late thirties. He had a mole on his chin.

'Make sure they're given a ride home in a squad car.'

Jerry nodded.

'And keep the reporters away from them.'

'Okay, Ira. But it won't be easy.'

To Graham and Connie, Preduski said, 'When you get home, unplug your telephones first thing. You'll have to deal with the press tomorrow. But that's soon enough. They'll be pestering you for weeks. One more cross to bear. I'm sorry. I really am. But maybe we can keep them away from you tonight, give you a few hours of peace before the storm.'

'Thank you,' Connie said.

'Now, I've got to be going. Work to do. Things that ought to have been done long ago. I'm always behind in my work. Always. I'm not cut out for this job. That's the truth.'

He shook hands with Graham and performed an awkward half bow in Connie's direction.

As he walked across the lobby, his wet shoes squished and squeaked.

Outside, he dodged some reporters and refused to answer the questions of others.

His unmarked car was at the end of a double line of police sedans, black-and-whites, ambulances and press vans. He got behind the wheel, buckled his safety belt, started the engine.

His partner, Detective Daniel Mulligan, would be busy inside for a couple of hours yet. He wouldn't miss the car.

Humming a tune of his own creation, Preduski drove onto Lexington, which had recently been plowed. There were chains on his tires; they crunched in the snow and sang on the few bare patches of pavement. He turned the corner, went to Fifth Avenue, and headed downtown.

Less than fifteen minutes later, he parked on a tree-lined street in Greenwich Village.

He left the car. He walked a third of a block,

keeping to the shadows beyond the pools of light around the street lamps. With a quick backward glance to be sure he wasn't observed, he stepped into a narrow passageway between two elegant townhouses.

The roofless walkway ended in a blank wall, but there were high gates on both sides. He stopped in front of the gate on his left.

Snowflakes eddied gently in the still night air. The wind did not reach down here, but its fierce voice called from the rooftops above.

He took a pair of lock picks from his pocket. He had found them a long time ago in the apartment of a burglar who had committed suicide. Over the years there had been rare but important occasions on which the picks had come in handy. He used one of them to tease up the pins in the cheap gate lock, used the other pick to hold the pins in place once they'd been teased. In two minutes he was inside.

A small courtyard lay behind Graham Harris's house. A patch of grass. Two trees. A brick patio. Of course, the two flower beds were barren during the winter; however, the presence of a wrought-iron table and four wrought-iron chairs made it seem that people had been playing cards in the sun just that afternoon.

He crossed the courtyard and climbed three steps to the rear entrance.

The storm door was not locked.

As delicately, swiftly and silently as he could manage, he picked the lock on the wooden door.

He was dismayed by the ease with which he had gained entry. Wouldn't people *ever* learn to buy good locks?

Harris's kitchen was warm and dark. It smelled

of spice cake, and of bananas that had been put out to ripen and were now overripe.

He closed the door soundlessly.

For a few minutes he stood perfectly still, listening to the house and waiting for his eyes to adjust to the darkness. Finally, when he could identify every object in the kitchen, he went to the table, lifted a chair away from it, put the chair down again without making even the faintest noise.

He sat down and took his revolver from the shoulder holster under his left arm. He held the gun in his lap.

44

The squad car waited at the curb until Graham opened the front door of the house. Then it drove away, leaving tracks in the five-inch snowfall that, in Greenwich Village, had not yet been pushed onto the sidewalks.

He switched on the foyer light. As Connie closed the door, he went into the unlighted living room and located the nearest table lamp. He turned it on – and froze, unable to find the strength or the will to remove his fingers from the switch.

A man sat in one of the easy chairs. He had a gun.

Connie put one hand on Graham's arm. To the man in the chair, she said, 'What are *you* doing here?'

Anthony Prine, the host of *Manhattan at Midnight*, stood up. He waved the gun at them. 'I've been waiting for you.'

'Why are you talking like that?' Connie asked.

'The Southern accent? I was born with it. Got rid of it years ago. But I can recall it when I want. It was losing the accent that got me interested in mimicry. I started in show business as a comic who did imitations of famous people. Now I imitate Billy James Plover, the man I used to be.'

'How did you get in here?' Graham demanded.

'I went around the side of the house and broke a window.'

'Get out. I want you out of here.'

'You killed Dwight,' Prine said. 'I drove by the Bowerton Building after the show. I saw all the cops. I know what you did.' He was very pale. His face was lined with strain.

'Killed who?' Graham asked.

'Dwight. Franklin Dwight Bollinger.'

Perplexed, Graham said, 'He was trying to kill us.'

'He was one of the best people. One of the very best there ever was. I did a program about vice cops, and he was one of the guests. Within minutes we knew we were two of a kind.'

'He was the Butcher, the one who –'

Prine was extremely agitated. His hands were shaking. His left cheek was distorted by a nervous tic. He interrupted Connie and said, 'Dwight was *half* the Butcher.'

'Half the Butcher?' Connie said.

Graham lowered his hand from the switch and gripped the pillar of the brass table lamp.

'I was the other half,' Prine said. 'We were identical personalities, Dwight and I.' He took one step toward them. Then another. 'More than that. We were incomplete without each other. We were halves of the same organism.' He pointed the pistol at Graham's head.

'Get out of here!' Graham shouted. 'Run, Connie!' And as he spoke he threw the lamp at Prine.

The lamp knocked Prine back into the easy chair.

Graham turned to the foyer.

Connie was opening the front door.

As he followed her, Prine shot him in the back.

A terrible blow on the right shoulder blade, a burst of light, blood spattering the carpet all around him . . .

He fell and rolled onto his side in time to see Ira Preduski come out of the hallway that led to the kitchen.

He floated on a raft of pain in a sea that grew darker by the second. What was happening?

The detective shouted at Prine and then shot him in self-defense. Once. In the chest.

The talk-show host collapsed against a magazine rack.

Pain. Just the first twitches of pain.

Graham closed his eyes. Wondered if that was the wrong thing to do. If you go to sleep, you'll die. Or was that only with a head injury? He opened his eyes to be on the safe side.

Connie was wiping the sweat from his face.

Kneeling beside him, Preduski said, 'I called an ambulance.'

Some time must have passed. He seemed to fade out in the middle of one conversation and in on the middle of the next.

He closed his eyes.

Opened them.

'Medical examiner's theory,' Preduski said. 'Sounded crazy at first. But the more I thought about it . . .'

'I'm thirsty,' Graham said. He was hoarse.

'Thirsty? I'll bet you are,' Preduski said.

'Get me . . . drink.'

'That might be the wrong thing to do for you,' Connie said. 'We'll wait for the ambulance.'

The room spun. He smiled. He rode the room as if it were a carousel.

'I shouldn't have come here alone,' Preduski said miserably. 'But you see why I thought I had to? Bollinger was a cop. The other half of the Butcher might be a cop too. Who could I trust? Really. Who?'

Graham licked his lips and said, 'Prine. Dead?'

'I'm afraid not,' Preduski said.

'Me?'

'What about you?'

'Dead?'

'You'll live.'

'Sure?'

'Bullet wasn't near the spine. Didn't puncture any vital organ, I'll bet.'

'Sure?'

'*I'm* sure,' Connie said.

Graham closed his eyes.

Epilogue
SUNDAY

Ira Preduski stood with his back to the hospital window. The late afternoon sun framed him in soft gold light. 'Prine says they wanted to start racial wars, religious wars, economic wars . . .'

Graham was lying on his side in the bed, propped up with pillows. He spoke somewhat slowly because of the pain killers he had been given. 'So they could gain power in the aftermath.'

'That's what he says.'

From her chair at Graham's bedside, Connie said, 'But that's crazy. In fact, didn't Charles Manson's bunch of psychos kill all those people for the same reason?'

'I mentioned Manson to Prine,' Preduski said. 'But he tells me Manson was a two-bit con man, a cheap sleazy hood.'

'While Prine is a superman.'

Preduski shook his head sadly. 'Poor Nietzsche. He was one of the most brilliant philosophers who ever lived – and also the most misunderstood.' He bent over and sniffed at an arrangement of flowers that stood on the table by the window. When he looked up again, he said, 'Excuse me for asking. It's none of my business. I know that. But I'm a curious man. One of my faults. But - when's the wedding?'

'Wedding?' Connie said.

'Don't kid me. You two are getting married.'

Confused, Graham said, 'How could you know that? We just talked about it this morning. Just the two of us.'

'I'm a detective,' Preduski said. 'I've picked up clues.'

'For instance?' Connie said.

'For instance, the way the two of you are looking at each other this afternoon.'

Delighted at being able to share the news, Graham said, 'We'll be married a few weeks after I'm released from the hospital, as soon as I have my strength back.'

'Which he'll need,' Connie said, smiling wickedly.

Preduski walked around the bed, looked at the bandages on Graham's left arm and on the upper right quarter of his back. 'Every time I think of all that happened Friday night and Saturday morning, I wonder how you two came out of it alive.'

'It wasn't much,' Connie said.

'Not much?' Preduski said.

'No. Really. It wasn't so much, what we did, was it, Nick?'

Graham smiled and felt very good indeed. 'No, it wasn't much, Nora.'